For
Young Mike
Hoping he will grow up to
appreciate a good Western

BITTER TRAIL

by

Erle Russell

The Golden West Large Print Books
Long Preston, North Yorkshire,
BD23 4ND, England.

British Library Cataloguing in Publication Data.

Russell, Erle
    Bitter trail.

        A catalogue record of this book is
        available from the British Library

        ISBN   978-1-84262-881-2 pbk

First published in Great Britain in 1954 by Hennel Locke Ltd.

Copyright © Erle Russell

Cover illustration © Gordon Crabb by arrangement with
Alison Eldred

The moral right of the author has been asserted

A catalogue record for this book is available from the British
Library

Published in Large Print 2013 by arrangement with
Erle Russell, care of Watson, Little Ltd.

The Golden West Large Print is an imprint of Library Magna
Books Ltd.

Printed and bound in Great Britain by
T.J. (International) Ltd., Cornwall, PL28 8RW

CONTENTS

Chapter One

STRANGER TO LORDVILLE

The rider sat his mount slackly. A weary bitterness etched itself in the lines of his tall figure, though the wide shoulders were now drooped, as the man's sombre gaze beat ahead through the descending curtain of dusk towards the distant cluster of buildings.

This, he thought, would be Lordville, the town which served the valley of the Creation River.

Lordville! Another two bit cow-town, like a thousand others he had seen during his wanderings over the last ten years.

He pushed back the dun-coloured stetson from thick black hair matted with sweat and trail-dust; for behind him lay sixty miles of desert.

Lean fingers spilled tobacco from the Bull Durham sack into brown paper and a dry tongue licked the gummed edge. A sulphur match flared in the purple-shadowed twilight and Lee Kells drew smoke down into his lungs, his thoughts bleak, his hard eyes on the blossoming yellow lights of the town yonder.

He reached forward and patted the paint

9

pony's dust and sweat-caked neck. The paint had carried him well to-day and the day before and the weeks before that and could use a rest. So could Kells. It was a tiring and frustrating chore, this searching for the killer of his father. A chore which already had taken him most of the preceding ten years.

He had been eleven when his father died, now, at a little over twenty-one, he was old for his age. Old with the cynicism of experience and embittered before his time by the evil and terrible thing he had witnessed ten years back. Sometimes the trail had run hot, other times it had gone cold to the point of non-existence.

No physical trail was this. No material and definite tracks to follow. Just a chance word dropped here or there, in a saloon maybe, or in a mining camp or round some outlying camp-fire in the wilderness.

A word or a description; a vague mention of some man and his habits, which, added to the knowledge Kells already possessed might quite well point the finger to where Frank Shards was now, ten years after that memorable night...

Kells dragged on his cigarette and watched night descend over Creation Valley. Watched the flare of light brighten from the town by virtue of the contrasting darkness all around.

How many more such towns would he approach, he wondered, and speculate on?

10

How many more trails would he ride with Red, his pony, and how many more hills would he ascend and descend to ascertain what lay beyond?

Quien sabe? as the Mexicans would say. Who can tell?

Presently, he stubbed out the cigarette on the smooth saddlehorn, spinning the dead stub into the darkness and lifting Red's reins.

A bare half hour later he was riding down Lordville's Main Street, his gaze probing the shadowed board-walks, seeking for someone whom he doubted he would recognize anyway.

Stores and saloons gave out their yellow light from hanging coal-oil lamps.

Folks, mostly men, drifted along the roofed-in walks. Noise issued from batwing doors like a physical thing, so that a man felt that his ear-drums had been hit.

Kells' searching gaze found the painted sign, made visible, and readable, by the lights cascading from Roper's Saloon. The legend read, 'Livery and Feed Barn. John Villiers. Prop.'

Kells kneed the horse towards the wide entrance on the corner of the first intersection, negotiating the evening traffic with an ease born of long practice.

Inside, the lamps glowed on golden straw and the glossy backs of ponies in their stalls and Kells, selecting an empty stall, stripped the paint, slinging the saddle and blanket across a saw-horse and hanging the concho-decorated bridle from a hook on the wall.

He had withdrawn the carbine from the scabbard when he became aware of the man behind him.

Everything about John Villiers was square-cut, though years, coupled with little activity, had tended to add a softening roundness to the original square-cut pattern and shape of the man.

His hair was iron-grey and not yet thinned to the point where his scalp would show through. His blue eyes twinkled behind the thick folds of his eyelids. A grey, longhorn moustache swept down over his mouth giving an air of faint melancholy to his face, now belied by the sparkle of interest in his eyes as his gaze switched from the pony to its owner.

'Howdy, stranger.' John Villiers' voice rumbled its greeting to the tall, grim-visaged, dusty rider. 'That's sure a nice pony you got, but it'll still cost a dollar for feed an' a night's lodging.' The smile accompanying the words took away any possible sting.

Lee Kells' face softened slightly. It was the nearest he got to a grin.

'I'm not grumbling, Villiers. In fact I'd figure on paying more if Red's to be rubbed down and groomed properly. Feel like I could do with a good rub down myself.'

'You come in across the desert?' Villiers'

eyes were wary as he asked the question. It was not always smart to ask what direction a man came from or in which direction he was figuring to travel, but the stranger nodded amiably for all his grim appearance.

'Name's Kells,' he said, 'Lee Kells. Reckon this'll be Lordville, Creation Valley country.'

The hostler agreed it was. He took two cigars from the pocket of his calf-skin vest, stuck one in his mouth and handed the other to Kells. After the smokes were lit, Villiers carefully blew out the match and placed the dead stick in his pocket.

'Don't you worry about that cayuse,' Villiers said and Kells smiled for the first time, knowing that the hostler was not using the word 'cayuse' in any uncomplimentary way. 'Cayuse,' usually meant an Indian pony, and they were often 'paints,' but although wiry, frequently were of poor stock. Kells' mount had the shape and proportion of a blood-stock pony and anyone with an eye to horse-flesh could see that, in spite of the dust and sweat that caked the animal.

The men drew away from the stalls, puffing blue smoke from the fragrant cigars.

'Where can I clean up and get a meal, Villiers?' Kells asked as they stood outside the hostler's lamp-lit office.

'The barber-shop, one block down, 'll fix you a bath and a shave. After that,' Villiers said, 'you could try Roper's Saloon, but the

13

drinks are better'n the grub there. If you want some real good home cookin', you cain't do better'n Starr's Restaurant right across the street from here.'

Kells thanked the likeable livery man and shoved a silver dollar into his hand as an advance against putting up the horse.

Slowly he came out on to the board-walk, transferring the cigar to his mouth and easing the six-gun in its holster on his right side before taking up the carbine.

He found the barber-shop without difficulty and less than an hour later emerged feeling fresh and invigorated. He knotted the clean bandana around his bronzed throat, hefting the rifle into the crook of his left arm, and crossing the dusty, noisy, shadow-filled street to the opposite board-walk.

He noted the sign which declared that, inside, the finest home-cooking this side of the Mississippi might be obtained at reasonable prices.

This was Starr's restaurant. He had thought of it as 'Stars'; now he saw the name painted in small characters in the bottom right-hand corner of the board. 'Marion Starr, Proprietress.'

This promised well, he thought, unfastening the screen-door and entering the half-filled room. In the West, particularly on ranches, where most cooking was done by men 'hash-slingers,' it was a treat to run into

14

a place like this occasionally.

Kells selected a vacant corner table. He leaned the carbine against the wall and gave the room his brief, yet observing gaze.

He saw mostly ranchers, small men he figured, and a few waddies. One of the latter, in particular, had the stamp of a foreman or *segundo* at least, belonging to a biggish spread. He had noted several horses racked outside in front of the restaurant and had subconsciously absorbed the Arrow brand on rump and shoulder.

Kells placed this lean, hatchet-faced man with the piercing black eyes as the probable *segundo* or ramrod of the Arrow Spread; no doubt a ranch somewhere along the floor of Creation Valley.

He was aware now of the waitress standing before him. Yet apart from the clean gingham apron, which partially covered the well-cut linsey dress, there was little to show that this girl, or woman, was a waitress.

She flushed under his cold appraisal, misreading the look in his eyes. She shivered slightly and the word 'deadly' sprang to her mind as she looked into the sun-blackened face and the cold grey eyes of this stranger to Lordville.

'What will you have?' she asked him quickly. 'Steak, fried potatoes, apple-pie, coffee? Or we can cook, bacon–.' Her words were interrupted by the sudden harsh shout

15

of the black-eyed, hatchet-faced man across the room.

'Hey! Marion! Git a move on will yuh with thet pie yuh was going to bring. An' rustle us up some more cawfee!'

Kells noticed the deep flush which stained the woman's face, spreading to the pale column of her neck. His glance moved over the man at the far table and in Kells' eyes was the coldness of ice.

'Better wait your turn, mister.' Kells' voice was soft, yet it cut through the conversation like a knife cutting butter.

The man's eyes turned even blacker and underneath the saddle-leather skin of his neck, a pulse beat angrily.

He half rose from his chair but a sandy-haired puncher sitting next him thrust out a long arm and forced him back.

Kells coolly waited to see whether the man would start something but apparently the sandy-haired puncher had persuaded him against any aggressive action for the moment.

'That's George Schillinger, foreman of the Arrow Spread,' Marion Starr whispered, bending over the table to straighten table napkin and carafe of water. 'Don't tangle with him, mister, whatever you do. I'll be right back with the food.'

But Kells saw presently that Marion Starr took fresh wedges of apple pie and more coffee to Schillinger's table before bringing over the steak and potatoes.

He looked at the woman again and felt a faint stirring of interest; almost sympathy. There was fear in back of her wide green-grey eyes and her face was pale, now that it had lost its flush of embarrassment.

The linsey dress she wore under the apron had small puffed sleeves, revealing soft shapely arms almost to the shoulders. Kells noted, almost without realizing it, the full roundness of her figure underneath the tight-waisted, ankle-length dress.

Her chestnut-coloured hair gleamed in the light from hanging lamps as she moved quickly amongst the tables, taking food, clearing away, and anticipating such things as requests for water or coffee.

Once, from the region of the kitchen in back of the restaurant, Kells caught sight of a young girl of about fifteen or so, obviously helping the male cook whose voice could be heard now and again as he repeated the various orders and plonked dishes on the counter near the entrance to the kitchen.

Kells finished his meal and rolled a cigarette, lighting it as Marion Starr approached with a cup of coffee.

Schillinger, together with the sandy-haired puncher who, Kells could now see, was taller even than the ramrod, had tromped across the restaurant, leaving money on the counter.

As Schillinger passed near to Kells' table,

he caught the girl around the fleshy part of her upper arm.

Kells could see the white marks when Schillinger drew his hand away. Lee Kells sat quite still. He wanted no part of anyone's troubles. Just as soon as the pony and himself were rested he was pushing on to Hide City. Hide City! That was the place where someone like Frank Shards had been seen six months ago.

Schillinger's voice grated through Kells' thoughts.

'See yuh later, Marion, so don't go to bed jest yet!' He guffawed loudly and for a brief moment Kells was tempted to smash his fist into that lean, evil-looking face. With an effort he controlled himself and in another moment, Schillinger and his companion had left the restaurant.

Talk, which had been soft and subdued, now sprang up and lifted to a crescendo. There was the relief of eased tension in the air. It was as though everyone had been scared to talk or even think while the Arrow men had been eating. Kells wondered what sort of men Arrow employed who could hold down a roomful of people without any effort. He knew the answer at once. George Schillinger, for all that he was a supposedly respectable foreman, was a killer. It was as clear to Kells as though the man were rubber-stamped.

He stirred his coffee slowly and shrugged. What the hell! By to-morrow Lordville and all its inhabitants would be on his back-trail. A spot on the map like many another he had passed through and left behind during the last ten years.

He stood on the board-walk, wondering why in hell he had not left the carbine with John Villiers at the livery. He hefted it now and began threading his way through the press of evening traffic. Men, and a few painted percentage girls on the walks or at the entrance to the saloons; saddle-horses spring-wagons and one-two buggies on the dusty street, all forming an ever-changing kaleidoscope of pattern and colour.

He passed 'Dell's Deck Saloon,' 'The Red Ox,' 'The Last Chance' and found Roper's Saloon a block down.

He pushed at the batwing doors, walking slowly towards the bar, watching, looking and dragging his gaze away from the sea of faces in front of him.

He called for whisky and found himself next to a smallish, mild-looking man whose sheriff's star partly showed from underneath his black vest.

Kells lowered his drink and poured a fresh one. The sheriff said, 'Figger on stayin' long in Lordville?'

Kells knew that the lawman had a perfect

right to question him thus, but the man's manner and appearance vaguely irritated him.

'No longer than it takes me to rest myself and my horse after crossing that furnace desert,' he said shortly.

But the sheriff was not to be put off. 'I'm Race Arnold,' he said. 'I'd admire to know your handle, stranger.'

'Lee Kells from San Saba, Waco, Dallas, Austin, San Antonio, San Angelo and most places west of the Sabine and not wanted in any – yet.' Kells concluded softly.

Arnold's face creased slightly into a grin. 'I didn't want your life history son. It's just a part of my job to look at strangers when they hit town. Me, I don't look for trouble, no sir. Have a drink on me, Kells.'

Lee's hard mood softened at the outer edges. It was not that all men were his enemies, not by a jugful. But this questing after old Ezra Kells' murderer – or at least the leader of the lynch mob – was something which consumed Lee's whole being. He had little time or room for anything else. Maybe it was a wrong attitude, but it was something which Kells could not help, even whilst recognizing that single-mindedness and selfishness could be the same thing under different names.

That was the one thing Lee Kells was gambling on after all these years; that however much a man changed in appearance, in his way of life, his place of living, or the mere altering of his name, he was still, intrinsically, the same man motivated by the same instincts. Kells figured that wherever Frank Shards was at this moment, whatever he called himself, he would still be, deep down, the same arrogant, thrusting and unscrupulous man he had been ten years back when he had swayed the other two-bit nesters into making a goat of Ezra Kells and had thrown him to the pack. Kells now accepted the sheriff's hospitality as he idly watched the two barkeeps serve up beer and whisky for thirsty, eager men.

'What kind of spread is Arrow, Sheriff?' he asked.

Race Arnold smiled. 'So you've heard of Arrow already, huh? Well, cain't say I'm surprised. She sure is the biggest spread in the whole of Creation an' Frank Shane–'

'Frank *who?*'

'Why, Frank Shane, I said. He's the owner of Arrow and like I was saying, he's a big man. Runs most o' the valley and the town.'

Race Arnold saw the surprise in the other man's eyes.

'Oh, it doesn't bother me, jest so long as Frank or any of his riders don't step too far over the line. Schillinger's the worst, I reckon; he's ramrod. Have a plumb difficult time keepin' that one from bustin' the traces.'

'I just met him,' Kells said softly, 'over to Starr's restaurant. We had a few words–'

There was a flicker of something in Race Arnold's eyes.

'Say, Kells. You wanta be a mite careful of George Schillinger. He's a gun-handy *hombre* if ever there was one. Reckon I don't cotton on to that killer brand, but he's steered careful up to now.'

Kells said, not caring much, 'So this Frank Shane runs Creation and Lordville and has got you in his pocket?'

A slow stain of colour deepened the mottled surface of the sheriff's face. 'Go easy, youngster,' he said quietly. 'I don't take that kind of talk from any folk, least of all–'

Kells turned on him then and Arnold watched the grey eyes glitter in the sun-blackened face, watched with careful interest but without alarm.

'You don't take that talk, Arnold, because it's true and we both know it. This Frank Shards–'

'Shane.'

'–Frank Shane, yeah, I kind of forgot. He must be quite a bucko,' Kells said. 'He–'

Lee's words were cut off by the gentle nudging of someone close to him at the bar. He had not heard anyone approach and now, for a moment, he was mystified until he looked down and saw a young girl trying

22

to insinuate her slight body between himself and the man next him.

He recognized her now, with something of a start. This was the girl he had seen peeping out from the kitchen at Marion Starr's restaurant. Here, close at hand, he saw the resemblance. She had the same red-tinted hair and grey eyes though the nose was freckled and the mouth wide to the point of being large.

She was gawky now, perhaps. In a few years she would be as beautiful as her mother. With sharp surprise, Kells realised that he had not thought of Marion Starr as a married woman and mother.

The girl gained the attention of one of the barkeeps. He grinned at her in friendly fashion and brought up a sealed bottle of whisky. She thrust the money into his hands and, hugging the bottle to her chest, scuttled out of the saloon.

Some of the men grinned, others showed frank disgust in their seamed faces, particularly the older men.

'That's Lettie,' Race Arnold told Kells by way of explanation. 'Lettie Harte, Marion's sister–'

'*Sister?*'

'Yep. Guess Marion herself ain't much older than her kid sister, maybe five-six years, even though she is a widow.'

Surprise gave way to surprise as Kells

absorbed these new facts which the sheriff offered.

'But isn't it kind of illegal for a kid to come in here, a young girl–?'

Arnold smiled, but this time without mirth.

'We all know it ain't for her, or Marion Starr,' he said. 'This George Schillinger I was tellin' you about – Arrow's ramrod – is kinda sparkin' Marion Starr, or so he figgers–'

'What happened, then in the past, Arnold? You say Marion Starr is a widow?'

The sheriff nodded. 'Last fall it was and her and Len Starr only married a few months. Not that Len was much either, but plumb better'n George Schillinger at that.

'I wasn't around when it happened but Schillinger had some sorta ruckus with Len. Both drew and Len got kilt all right. Witnesses, most on 'em anyway, swore Len drew fust and that George only acted in self-defence. That's what the coroner's findin's was and after that the thing was finished.

'It wasn't until later I got round to thinkin' most o' the witnesses was Arrow men anyway, but there wasn't a durn thing I could do about it. Like I said, I never saw the shootin' and the main consensus of opinion was that Schillinger drew after Len and only shot in self-defence.'

Kells rolled and lit another cigarette. For a

long time he remained silent. Again he reminded himself of his ever-present chore. This was not his piece of grief. Let well alone. Shake the dust of Lordville from his feet.

Yet he could not entirely forget the face and form of Marion Starr. Her image seemed to swim in front of him, nebulous, yet clear, against the background of moving men in Roper's saloon.

He saw the chestnut brown hair tied back at the nape of her neck, red lights gleaming in it as she moved back and forth in his mental picture. He saw the soft curve of her cheek and the bright red lips and under the thick brows, the wide grey eyes in back of which lurked the haunting reflection of fear.

He turned abruptly, spinning a coin on to the counter.

'Hey!' Arnold called. 'Where you figger on goin' at such a hell of a lick?'

'Starr's Restaurant,' Kells said over his shoulder.

With a sudden movement, half-resolve, half-resignation, Race Arnold downed his drink, hitched up his belt and followed the stranger to Lordville out into the night.

Chapter Two

A CHALLENGE

Time had sped by on hurrying feet, Kells saw when he came out on to the board-walk. The traffic had thinned somewhat and there were fewer folk on this main street. Stores had all closed long ago and now the only lights were those streaming from saloons and such places as Starr's Restaurant.

Kells crossed the street with long, measured strides. Dust stirred around his boots and the long-rowelled Texas spurs left their separate tracks.

He hauled up outside Marion Starr's place, every instinct in him whispering for him to be gone and on his way; not to tangle with things and people that were not his concern.

It was the same stubborn streak which had kept Kells on the trail of Frank Shards for so long that now brushed aside the small voices of protest.

He pushed open the door only half aware that the sheriff had followed him across the street.

In the far corner of the room a man was seated at a table, his head in his arms. Only

26

afterwards did Kells realize that this was the sandy-haired pard of Arrow's ramrod.

Nearer to the counter, Schillingner lounged in a chair at a table on which were glasses and bottles of whisky. Lettie cowered in a corner, her face white with fright. Schillinger had his arm around Marion's slim waist, the easy strength of the man forcing her on to his thighs. Already the shoulder of her dress had become torn and disarranged so that the white flesh of her bosom was partly revealed.

Like her kid sister's, Marion's face was as white as chalk. Her red lips showed up oddly against the pale surround of her cheeks. Her hair too had become unpinned and was falling half across her face.

One moment Schillinger tried to force her to drink some whisky, the next, his saddle-leather face was reaching up to kiss her tightly drawn mouth. All this Kells saw in a matter of seconds. Without conscious thought, he crossed the room, knocking over chairs as he went. A vice-like hand gripped the front of George Schillinger's shirt so that he was dragged up on to his feet before he could focus on what was happening. Marion was sent half sprawling against the counter as the Arrow ramrod released her to deal with this sudden and unexpected onslaught.

He rocked back as Kells' fist caught him on the cheek bone, but the blow sobered him rather than robbed him of his senses.

27

He swept the table away with his left hand as though it were so much matchwood, aiming a surprisingly swift blow to Kells' belly and coming in fast with a left and another looping right which caught Kells full in the teeth.

Lee spat blood and at least one tooth. He shook his head to clear it and sank a swift left and right into the ramrod's body. Schillinger doubled up with pain, gasping for breath, half-retching. He sent another looping blow at Kells' face which Lee avoided so that Schillinger's fist shot over his shoulder, grazing his ear.

Now the ramrod was thrown violently against the other man by the impetus of the blow, but instead of drawing back he brought his knee up into Kells' belly, low down.

Lee felt sick. There was no breath in his lungs and a horrible feeling in his stomach. He rode another blow from the ramrod, playing for time, striving to regain his breath. Schillinger stepped back a pace, measuring his distance and stumbled against a chair.

Then Kells went forward. Both men's shirts were half torn to the waist and sweat shone wetly on their faces. Kells' left fist sank into Schillinger's stomach. He followed this with a right to the ramrod's heart. Now Kells was using him like a punch-bag. A berserk fury had caught hold of the stranger to Lordville.

He had been almost whipped a few moments ago by that dirty foul. Now, all he wanted to do was to hurt this drunken swine and beat him into unconsciousness.

He kept on, now hammering at the sagging body, now transferring his raw knuckles to the man's glazed and bloody face. Schillinger was almost out on his feet, but still he wouldn't go down and still Kells refused to stop.

Then Lee stepped back, putting the whole weight of his two hundred and ten pounds behind the force of that last rocking blow to the jaw.

Schillinger folded then, hitting the floor so hard that he slid along until coming to a stop at the base of the counter.

Kells stood over him, chest heaving, eyes half-filled with sweat, and blood in his mouth and nostrils.

He became aware of a noise behind him. Sudden shouts. He turned slowly, stupidly. The man at the table was awake now, the sandy-haired one. There were other riders in the room. Rough-and-tumble men by the look of things. These men are Arrow, Kells thought bleakly and then understood why they had not moved against him.

Race Arnold stood just inside the door to the left, a six-shooter trained on the five Arrow men.

'Get that drunken bum outa here before I

clap the whole lot of you in jail an' charge you with disturbin' the peace, wilful damage and attempted murder an' anything else I can think up.

'Go on, I say! You, Schultz and you, Denkern, clear that mess of a ramrod off'n the floor and get to hell outa here. Kessel! You see they do like I say. Get back to Arrow. You come back, any of you, an' I'll throw you in jail, pronto.'

Kessel's eyes smouldered but he did what he was told.

'Pick George up boys and get him on his pony.' To Arnold he said. 'Watch out, Sheriff, you don't get so big Frank has to cut you down. We'll be in town to-morrow. Better go easy.'

Kells, wiping his face and hands on his neckerchief, said, 'There sure is a stink of polecats around here.'

Flip Denkern's gaze rested briefly on the battle-scarred face of the stranger.

'I don't know who you are, brother, but whoever you are, ef'n you value your hide, you'd best light a shuck outa Creation by sun-up.'

'Get movin'!' Race Arnold rasped, and Kells wondered where the softly-spoken, mild-mannered sheriff had disappeared to.

In less than five minutes the room was empty, save for Arnold, Kells, Lettie and Marion.

Presently Kells found himself in the rear part of the building.

In back of the restaurant was a large kitchen as he had surmised and here was a large sink with a pump. Beyond, he caught a glimpse of other rooms leading off from a small corridor.

Marion was sloshing water into the sink before filling a kettle which she placed on the stove. Arnold had fed wood to the stove, and Lettie, recovered somewhat from her scare, placed a coffee-pot beside the kettle.

'You can get the worst off at the sink,' Marion said. 'In a moment I'll bathe your cuts and bruises with warm water.'

Kells only nodded. It was difficult to talk now that his lips were so swollen and bleeding. He felt as though every tooth in his head were loose, but a closer inspection proved that he had lost but one.

Race Arnold rather self-consciously holstered his gun. He glanced towards Marion who went into one of the further rooms, then switched his gaze to Lettie.

'Suppose Gil Rabjohn had gone off for the night, Lettie, else he might've given you some help?'

Lettie nodded. 'He allus figgers on going when we're getting ready to close up. Any cooking to be done after ten, Marion does it.'

Kells groped for and found the towel,

dabbing his face and hands now smarting painfully from the whiplash blows of George Schillinger's fists. At least now he could see more clearly and begin to take in what was going on.

'Rabjohn's your cook and day-man, Lettie?' he said. The girl nodded and Arnold said, 'Reckon these girls need to have a man about the place when scum like Schillinger's in town.'

Shortly, Marion returned, her dress re-arranged and fastened temporarily at the shoulders. There was a little more colour in her face. She even contrived a smile.

'Now, let me look to your wounds, Mr–'

'Kells,' he murmured. 'Lee Kells, and I guess I know you're Marion Starr and this is Lettie, your kid sister.'

She nodded, indicating a chair near the kitchen table. Kells sat down and Marion bathed his face with the warm water, after-wards applying unguents to the worst of the places. When she had finished Kells didn't look so bad. He grinned at himself in the mirror.

'Thanks, Miss Starr – huh – Mrs Starr, I reckon–'

'You know about me, Mr Kells?'

Race Arnold said, 'I gave him an outline, Marion, figgered you wouldn't object.'

'Object? I couldn't object to Mr Kells knowing anything about me. I was never so relieved in all my life as when he showed up and dealt with Schillinger.'

Lettie poured coffee and when Arnold had finished his he rose to go.

'I've got a few chores to see to, folks,' he told them, 'but I'll be around on the street for some time. Even so, I don't figure any of Arrow'll be back to-night.'

He nodded good-night and went out by way of the restaurant. Lettie followed to put the door on the latch and to start in on cleaning up some of the mess.

Kells sipped his coffee and rolled a cigarette. He was feeling the reaction now and his thoughts were going ahead once again to the main task in his life.

Already he was considering all this as just another incident on the way. Yet when he looked at the girl, he found her gaze on him, full of speculation and bright with interest.

'I reckon it would be difficult for me to thank you enough, Mr Kells, for what you did to-night. There aren't many men, none I guess around here, would tackle Schillinger. Certainly none who could have whipped him like you did.'

Kells placed the cigarette between his battered lips and smiled.

Marion Starr was more than surprised at the change in this man's face when he smiled. It was no longer hard and wooden and bitter. It was the face of a youngster, almost, until the bleak look came back once again and his grey eyes became cold.

She said softly. 'Lordville could use a man like you, Mr Kells. The whole valley for that matter.' She laughed apologetically. 'But why should I be worrying you with our problems, I guess you've got plenty of your own?'

He nodded. 'Enough to last me, Mrs Starr. I've been looking for my father's murderer for ten years. There's a million to one chance that he's in Hide City, or was. That's the last tip-off I received about six months ago.

'Reckon you'll understand why I am to leave for Hide City sun-up to-morrow?'

Horror and sympathy were mingling expressions in Marion Starr's wide-open eyes.

'Your father's murderer? But that's terrible. What happened? I mean–' she bit her lip. 'I guess it's not my business anyway. I didn't aim to be inquisitive...'

As he drank his coffee and smoked the cigarette, he began to tell her about it, feeling a great up-surging relief.

This thing had been bottled up far so long, locked tightly within his breast since a boy, that he felt now, as he talked, as though the burden had become lighter. As though he had found an ally and a friend. Yet, he thought, she was but a woman, herself needing friends and allies with Arrow running the town and valley and their riders, or at least the foreman, molesting her with his drunken wooing.

'I was only a button,' Kells said slowly, the light of dim and half-forgotten memories in his eyes. 'My pa was a nester, a good man, Mrs Starr, who believed in the Good Book and in doing good works. He kept himself poor by helping others.'

Kells broke off to smile bitterly.

'There were a few other nesters on this strip bordering the big Crockett spread in the San Saba Valley. Chief amongst them was a man called Frank Shards. Reckon he was about thirty then which'd make him forty or thereabouts now, if he's still alive.'

'What happened?' Marion Starr said softly.

Kells shrugged slightly. 'We were all shoe-string outfits, of course, running a few head each, mostly mavericks I guess which rightly belonged to Crockett.

'Shards got the others together and put up a plan to rustle some of Crockett's outlying beef. The range was so vast their riders couldn't possibly watch all the cattle. It was easy. But my pa, Ezra Kells, would have none of it. It was out-and-out stealing and I reckon he was right, although I didn't figure all this out at the time, of course.

'Shards and the others had told him the plan whereby they could lift fifty head each without Crockett knowing and pa not only refused but told them bluntly he was going to warn Crockett of what they planned.' Kells finished his coffee and silently Marion replenished the cup from the pot on the stove.

'Dad signed his own death-warrant when he told them what he figured to do. Trouble was he just wasn't scared of anyone. They fixed it then so that "rustled" cattle were found on our section. Crockett's beef and Frank Shards, the ringleader, egged on the others to lynch him—'

'They lynched your father?'

Kells nodded. 'They were scared he'd talk and tell Crockett the plan and spoil their chances for the future. With dad out of the way, they could still work their big steal.

'Reckon they might have done something about me, but I hid out in the thick mesquite and chaparral, near the cabin. I saw it all. I swore then and there to get the ringleader if it took me a lifetime. It was all Shards' doing. The others had no stomach for physical violence nor were they happy about doing this to Ezra Kells. He was a good man and those swine knew it.'

'Frank Shards,' Marion said slowly. 'What was he like, Lee?' She scarcely noticed that she had used Kells' first name, so absorbed was she in this story of frontier retribution.

'Guess I can't remember much about him except that he seemed pretty big to me in those days, but mebbe that was just a kid's view-point. Why, I guess he was kind of stocky and square with dark curly hair, close

36

cut. One thing I always remembered, he had a long white scar on the back of his right hand.'

Marion did not reply, but her eyes were unusually thoughtful as she watched Kells shrug into his calfskin vest, thus hiding most of the tears and slits in his shirt.

'Reckon I'll get some sleep,' he said extending his partially bandaged right hand. 'Thanks for fixing me up like you done – Marion.'

The faintest shade of madder-rose crept into her face as she smiled and gently took Lee's hand. 'It's I who should be doing the thanking, Lee. Like I said before. Where are you going to sleep to-night?'

Kells grinned and again Marion Starr was impressed by the transformation wrought by that infectious smile. 'John Villiers'll fix me up in his hayloft. I'd rather that than a flea-ridden broken-down hotel bed.'

Kells knew he had slept long beyond his normal time. The sun was streaming into the unglazed window of the hayloft over the livery and from somewhere below came the faint, deliciously provoking smell of coffee.

He rolled out of the blanket, brushed straw from his shirt and pants and winced as bruises and aching muscles made themselves suddenly felt.

He got to his feet, limbering up his body

and easing the stiffness from his joints, and glanced at the strips of bandage on his hands. He peeled off the covering across his right hand and found that the unguents Marion had used last night, had already gone a long way to healing the broken skin. As it so happened, his left hand was in the worst shape and this he left still partially covered. He flexed the fingers of his right hand, working the stiffness from them and drawing his gun and thumbing back the hammer several times until he was satisfied that, after all, there was no appreciable loss of his normal speed.

Presently he descended the ladder and made his way to the pump in the yard. The ice-cold water cleared his brain and wonderfully invigorated his bruised face and body.

Villiers called across from the office, 'I figured you'd best sleep on, son. That's why I didn't disturb you. There's a cup of cawfee here if you want.'

Kells grinned and waved his arm, vigorously towelling himself until his whole body glowed. Then he selected a fresh shirt from his war-bag in the stall, rolling the torn and bloody one into a ball and pitching it into a trash can.

He came across to the hostler's office and found a battered chair, gratefully accepting the proffered cup of steaming coffee.

'I'd figured to be well on my way by now,'

he told the liveryman, 'but I guess it don't much matter. I've got all the time in the world, anyway.'

Villiers said nothing. He merely nodded. If this man wanted to talk he would.

'Been ten years looking for a killer,' Kells said presently. 'Guess another few hours won't make no never-mind.'

Villiers did ask a question, then. 'You figger he's around these parts, someplace?'

Kells shrugged, place his coffee cup on the desk and shaped a cigarette.

'I heard that a man like this Frank Shards had been seen in Hide City. That was nearly six months ago. How far's this place anyway?'

'Right the other end of Creation Valley, son,' Villiers told him. ''bout sixty miles I suppose. Say a coupla days easy ride.'

Villiers sat down on an upturned crate. 'I wish you luck, anyway. Pity you cain't stay on in Lordville. The place sure needs some cleanin' up.'

Kells smiled. 'Why pick me for the job?'

The hostler shrugged. Any man who would handle Schillinger like you did last night – and I might tell you it's all over town – is the kind of man we could do with around here.'

Kells stood up. 'That's the second time I've had that said within a few hours. Marion Starr was the other.

'Well, John. I'll be on my way soon. You

might saddle up Red for me while I get breakfast.'

Villiers nodded shortly and tramped down the runway to the stalls as Lee turned, crossing Main at an angle to reach Starr's restaurant.

Lettie was serving late breakfasts and in her neat and freshly starched gingham apron and with her hair brushed sleekly back, she looked older than she had done last night as a white-faced, scared kid.

Kells, who had put on a jacket this morning, now slipped it off against the heat of the restaurant and proceeded to consume a large-sized breakfast.

He smoked one cigarette with his coffee and looking up suddenly, saw Marion at the counter.

He smiled at her, fishing into his gold-poke for money to pay for the meal and then transferring the change to his pants' pocket.

There were few people in the restaurant at this hour and Kells on a sudden impulse, took the girl's hand. A warm look came into her eyes before the lids dropped and the black lashes masked her secret thoughts.

'Look after yourself, Marion,' Kells said and, picking up his coat, swung round and out of the restaurant.

In a matter of minutes, he was astride the paint and moving out from Villiers' Livery on to Main Street.

He pointed his mount up-street towards the trail that led to Hide City, just as the rataplan of racing hoofs came suddenly and loudly to his ears.

Kells hauled up and turned his head, like everyone else on the street. Women were shopping, men were talking or purchasing stores but all stopped abruptly to pin-point the rider who had appeared in a cloud of dust at the other end of the street.

Kells heard folk exclaim. 'Looks like an Arrow rider' – 'What in tarnation's he burnin' leather like that for–?' 'Sure is in a hurry thet pilgrim. Looks like Phil Dukes.'

The rider astride his lathered horse had spotted Kells ahead.

Now he raced up and drew rein, his own lungs as well as his mount's working like bellows. On the board-walk folk watched and listened with open interest.

'George Schillinger says he's comin' in to get you, Kells. Says for you to look out for him some time to-day. That is ef'n you ain't too scared to meet him.'

There was a sudden hush in the ranks of the men and women on the side-walk. Now, all gazes shifted to the face of the stranger to Lordville. They waited almost breathlessly on his reply.

'Tell your drunken ramrod, I'll wait here in town until high noon,' Kells replied slowly and clearly. 'If he isn't here by then, I guess it'll be because he's too yellow–'

Phil Dukes' face darkened as his right hand moved towards the gun at his hip.

'Keep your hands away from your guns, friend,' Kells said. 'My quarrel isn't with you and it's sure inconveniencing me to have to hang about for Schillinger.

'Tell him before noon, else I'll be on my way.'

Phil Dukes nodded. As this man had said, the quarrel was not between them. Dukes was only the messenger, to deliver and take back whatever was said.

Now he neck-reined the lathered mount and trotted back towards the Arrow spread without even stopping off for a drink.

Kells slowly turned his horse back to the livery...

Chapter Three

DUEL AT HIGH NOON

The waiting would not affect Kells' nerves. He had none. But it was an irritating delay, nevertheless. He had told Villiers, the host-ler, that he had intended being on his way long before he had actually awakened this morning, whilst admitting that he had all

42

the time in the world for this self-imposed chore of trailing his father's murderer. Yet, when it came to delays of this kind, Kells felt cheated somehow and begrudged each previous moment as a miser begrudges parting with his gold.

But Lee Kells had never yet run from a fight and he had no intention of doing so now. He could but contain himself as patiently as possible and quietly await George Schillinger's arrival.

Kells was mildly surprised that George had made this challenge so soon after the fight and his beating up. But if Schillinger's gun-hand were not damaged, as apparently was the case, then the man would be at no disadvantage. A bruised body and a lacerated face need not necessarily prevent a fast and accurate draw and Kells, as he walked slowly towards Roper's saloon, wondered how Schillinger would play this lone hand.

A startling thought came suddenly, causing him to pause in mid-stride outside the saloon. Would Schillinger play a lone hand, or would he have other Arrow riders siding him?

Kells was conscious of the stare of folk on the sidewalk and the bright flicker of interest in the eyes of the men as he entered Roper's saloon. The impending duel was all over town. Bets were being laid, some openly, others in furtive fashion, as though somehow

Kells might disapprove of this kind of thing. He did! Not that betting worried him, but when men laid their money on the swiftness of a draw and benefited or lost as a result of a man being shot and perhaps killed, then Kells felt nothing but a bitter contempt, realising that none of these men who betted thus would stake their own lives on their gunhands or even on the fast draw of another man.

Lee called for whisky, searching the saloon for any sign of Race Arnold. He was wondering how the sheriff would stand in a thing like this. Last night, Arnold, a man who tacitly admitted his position was due to Arrow and its owner Frank Shane, had sided with Kells against Arrow. Had thrown a gun on Schillinger and his riders, threatening them with all kinds of penalties if they didn't get out of town fast.

Surely, Kells thought now, Arnold had a job to do as peace officer in stopping this gun fight that was to come before noon.

But Kells had the answer to this problem in a very few moments. Giff Roper himself came down and, seeing Kells, walked across to the counter.

He was a big man, hefty, without being fat. His black hair was slicked down with the fashionable cowlick. His face was brick-red and like his body, massive, even though bisected by a sweeping black moustache. He was as tall as Kells and wider. A big man.

'The drinks are on the house, Kells,' he said, extending a black-haired brawny hand. 'Any man who tangles with Schillinger and is prepared to back it up has my admiration.'

'Thanks,' Kells smiled. 'You wouldn't be trying to get me drunk, would you?'

Roper said, 'I ain't that kinda skunk, Kells. When you've finished with Schillinger, you can come back and have what you like. Until then, I'm limiting you to four drinks.'

'Fair enough,' Lee said and turned back to his whisky.

He felt Roper's hand on his arm and sensed something urgent in the big man's grip.

'You watch out for treachery, Kells. I'm telling you Schillinger's as dangerous as a rattler and as slippery as an eel. It wouldn't surprise me none if he tried to rig this play – in his favour, of course.'

Kells felt a tiny trickle of cold down his back now that Roper had put his own thoughts into words.

It was one thing to brace a man of Schillinger's repute. It was another to feel that somewhere behind you was another man lining his sights on your back.

'The thought did cross my mind,' Lee said, 'but thanks for the warning. I guess I'd better be on the look-out. Say, you any idea where Arnold is this morning?'

Giff Roper's lips curled under his flowing moustache. 'I guess he suddenly found some urgent business, plumb out of town. Reckon he ain't got the nerve to stop this fight and don't want any part of it. Still an' all,' Roper continued more tolerantly, 'Race Arnold's got a wife an' three kids. I guess I can understand. It's not so much he's scared of losing his job. But his family – you understand me, stranger?'

Kells nodded. He understood only too well. Race Arnold was a puppet like so many lawmen in the west and the strings were pulled by some one big. In this case, Arrow, meaning Frank Shane. Race Arnold was a likeable enough man and how he had gotten into this job, Lee didn't know. It was easy enough, anyway. Once in it, he had to jump as the strings were pulled. If he didn't – well, there was always his family as Giff Roper had implied.

Shortly, his quota of drinks finished, Lee stepped out on to the street. The rest of the time, now, he would stay outside, getting his eyes accustomed to the glare of the sun and figuring the best position to himself when Schillinger should ride into town.

Once, Kells drew his gun and spun the cylinder, checking the loads and the breech mechanism. He carefully lowered the hammer, thrust the gun back into its scabbard and slowly rolled a smoke. It was noticeable that as the forenoon crawled away, the board-walks became less frequented.

Then Kells saw the man from the corner of his eye! It was not Schillinger, but the face was familiar even in the brief glance he had before the man ducked out of sight down the alley opposite, between Villiers' feed barn and the Horseshoe Saloon.

Kells racked his brains, striving to recollect where he had seen that face. It might be important.

Suddenly he had it. The man had been with the other Arrow riders last night when they had all come tumbling into Marion Starr's restaurant to side Schillinger and the sandy-haired puncher.

The sheriff had thrown a gun on them and Kells himself had been pretty much occupied with Schillinger himself. But he had noticed the faces of the other men, even though only hazily, through the red mist of anger. Undoubtedly, the fellow who had ducked down the alley was an Arrow hand, and it came to Kells now that this might well be a part of the rigged play about which Roper had warned him and of which he had been suspicious himself.

When Kells looked again, some twenty minutes later, he caught sight of the man's shadow jutting out slightly from the alley. The tip of a hat brim was also just visible and Kells had a moment's panic as a rider hit Main Street some hundred yards up and became identified as George Schillinger. The time now was a quarter of twelve, and as Schillinger racked his horse down street, Kells' bleak glance swept over the now deserted street. He could see a few folk on the board-walks, mostly waiting tensely in doorways, or trying to lose themselves in the shadows. There were women as well as men and for a second Kells thought he caught sight of Marion Starr's white face looking at him. But he was not sure, and he could no longer afford to let outside things interfere with the business on hand.

Schillinger was coming towards him, walking slowly, hands hanging loosely an inch or so over the butts of his guns.

'All right, Kells. I'm coming for you!'

Lee stood and waited in the tense silence that followed the Arrow ramrod's challenge. He was watching Schillinger, but now and again his gaze darted sideways to where the shadow in the alley was edging ever nearer. The hatbrim was now more clearly visible and the third time Kells' narrowed gaze slanted in that direction he glimpsed the shine of steel as the sun glinted along the barrel of the man's six-gun.

Kells felt trapped, yet he did not make a move, preferring that Schillinger should be the one to go for his guns first. Now the ramrod's footfalls were clearly audible in the deathly silence which had built itself to fever pitch.

Dust stirred from Schillinger's high-heeled boots as he steadily advanced, his hat pulled well down over his eyes, his head thrust out from his hunched shoulders. The clawlike hands were brushing the butts of his six-guns.

Suddenly Schillinger's right hand dived down and came up filled with a gun. The men were a bare thirty yards away.

Kells fell forward into the dirt at the same instant that he drew his gun and fired, not at the spraddle-legged figure shooting ahead, but at the man who had momentarily emerged from the protection of the alley. His shot had come perilously close to killing Kells because he had fired even before Schillinger had completed his draw.

The bullet had gone clean through Kells' stetson, tugging it from his head. Now Lee swung his gun round and fired. The first slug sent chips of wood flying from the edge of the building, but before the man could dodge back, Lee's second shot triggered fast on top of the first, caught him full in the face! Kells' heard him scream even as another bullet from Schillinger's gun seared Kells's cheek, nicking the top of his left ear in its screaming flight.

All at once it seemed that guns were opening up everywhere around. Another shot

49

had been fired from Kells's right side this time and a little way behind. He ignored this, while he took careful aim at Schillinger. He fired then and saw the ramrod spin round and drop his gun. He stood for a few moments, clutching his side, tottering and staggering like a Saturday-night drunk. But even from this distance Lee could see the dark rich fluid beginning to squeeze itself between Schillinger's clutching fingers.

He went down then with a crash, stirring spurts of dust from the ground.

Everyone started shouting and Kells, still prone on the ground, put his gaze to the board-walk, seeing Marion Starr at the very edge, a smoking gun in her hand and a little distance away and behind, the prone body of yet another man.

Kells slowly picked himself up as men almost literally fell from the board-walk on to the street and started showering him with congratulations. They pointed out Marion Starr gleefully, each vying with the other in telling the story that had happened and describing the by-play which had gone on unknown to Lee Kells.

The man whom Kells had spotted in the alley was Foley Kessel and had, of course, been planted there by Schillinger. With most of the top of his head blown away he would now be 'planted' permanently. But Schillinger had had a second man on the scene. Luke Putnam. And he had managed to secrete himself near the blacksmith shop over to the other side without anyone at first detecting his presence.

It was Marion Starr who had seen the sinister figure move out from behind the cottonwood tree in front of the shop and she who had snatched at the holstered gun of a man standing close to her on the board-walk.

Before anyone could fathom what was happening, Marion had pointed the gun at Luke Putnam who was already aiming his own colt at the prone figure of Lee Kells.

The girl had fired once and missed, but it had been enough to deflect Putnam's aim and cause the man to wheel on her in a sudden paroxism of frustrated fury.

But Marion Starr had shot again. Twice, thrice she sent hot lead against that menacing figure by the tree and the third bullet had sent Luke Putnam crashing to the ground.

Folks came out now and crossed over to inspect the motionless figures of the Arrow men. Kells found that although Kessel and Putnam were both dead, Schillinger was only rather badly wounded. The bullet had not pierced his side, as Lee had at first thought, but had shattered his left arm.

Several men now picked him up and half-carried, half-walked him towards Doc Ivory's cottage on one of the side streets.

Kells wiped sweat from his face and found

the smear of blood where the bullet had scorched his cheek. He felt badly in need of a drink now and remembered Roper's promise. But first he must see Marion Starr. The girl who had saved his life and who had now been taken inside her own place by Gil Rabjohn, Marion's cook and handyman.

Once again Marion Starr's restaurant, and particularly the back kitchen, became a place for first-aid. In a little over twelve hours, Kells and the girl had again been thrown together and on both occasions, circumstances were such as to lend an intimacy to the scene which Lee tried stubbornly to resist.

Even though Marion Starr was unhurt, Kells noted that her face was still chalk-white and that her hands trembled in her lap. She sat at the kitchen table while Gil Rabjohn bustled about at the stove and carried the orders through into the restaurant. Lettie was already pouring thick, strong coffee into cups set on the table before them.

Lee thought he understood how bad Marion Starr was feeling. She had killed a man, undoubtedly the first human being she had ever killed or probably ever shot at. There was, most often, a terrible reaction to a thing like this. Even a man, like so many in the lawless west, who had killed a fellow being, however justly, could not always escape this sick feeling afterwards.

Lettie, after one anxious glance at the face of her elder sister, poured the coffee into the cups and turned back to the stove to give Gil what help she could.

Marion managed a wan smile and gratefully sipped the stimulating liquid while Kells watched her, as he built a smoke.

'Reckon I'm pretty much indebted to you, Marion,' he said slowly. 'I wouldn't be leaving town in an upright position if it hadn't been for your fast thinking, and straight shooting. Guess maybe you feel kind of sick at the moment, but it will pass. Like I said, if you hadn't killed this Luke Putnam I'd be a dead mackerel right now.'

She tried to smile. 'I'll be all right I guess, but it's the first time I've ever – but they were murderers, Mr Kells, murderers, and there seems to be no law around here to deal with this kind of thing–'

'There are a thousand and one places in the west where the only law is the gun a man wears on his hip,' Kells told her sympathetically. 'Until the time when cattle barons like the Arrow owner and his kind are brought into line, men – and women – will always have to be ready to defend themselves against attack.'

Marion Starr nodded. 'I hadn't spotted Foley Kessel. It was lucky you saw him. Still they were pretty long odds against you.'

Kells grinned and drank some coffee. 'You

evened things up somewhat. I guess I owe you plenty. If there's anything I can do–'

She opened her mouth to speak and then closed it again, shaking her head so that lights danced in the red-brown hair. 'I'm all right, Mr Kells, and I don't figure Frank Shane or Schillinger will hurt me because of this–'

'I could wish I'd killed that ramrod,' Kells said, the old, bleak look returning to his face. 'He'll be worrying you again before the month is out, if it's only a shattered arm he's got.'

He rose from the table, picking up his coat and slinging it over his left arm. He felt suddenly uncomfortable. He knew that this woman would like him to stay on in Lordville or at least in Creation Valley. She had saved his life and by rights there ought to be nothing which he would not do by way of recompense.

But this was the one thing which was impossible to do. To stay on her while Frank Shards the man chiefly responsible for Ezra Kells' death went free and unpunished as he had done so far these last ten years, was unthinkable.

Marion Starr stood up and took Kells's hand. 'I guess I know how you feel – Lee, and what you're thinking,' she smiled. 'Save it. You don't owe anyone here a thing. I reckon we're quits after last night.' She squeezed his fingers and dropped her arm to her side.

'Good luck, anyway,' she said, 'and I hope you find the man you're looking for.'

She watched the tall figure of Lee Kells as he walked slowly from the room, knowing that if she had wished she could have kept him here. There was quite a chance that Frank Shane, owner of Arrow, was indeed the man Kells was looking for. He answered to the description fairly accurately and Frank had a white scar on the back of his right hand.

Why then had she not told him this? Why was she even now letting this man go in the belief that his enemy was in Hide City?

Some stupid and irrational idea in back of her mind had held her from coming out into the open about Frank Shane, she now admitted to herself. A vague and shadowy idea, lacking logic as it lacked substance, had kept her mouth closed. She had not wanted Kells to go riding to Arrow against overwhelming odds, to brace Frank. Yet, she told herself now with a bitter smile, he was on the way to Hide City for just such a purpose. And suppose Frank Shane, after all were not the man Kells was hunting? Suppose Lee found this Shards in Hide City after all? If that were so she had not saved Kells anything. He would still fight it out with the man he trailed, once face to face with him, whatever the odds. He had not baulked at the odds today, even though he had known about Foley

Kessel. Lee Kells, Marion thought, was not the man to baulk at any odds or climb down if he figured he were in the right.

She might have saved trouble in Creation Valley, but she had not saved Kells from trouble.

Now she passed through the half-empty restaurant and came out on to the shaded walk. She saw him then, the silhouette of horse and rider rendered small by distance. Yet she knew it was Kells on his way out of Lordville and taking the trail to Hide City.

Perhaps after all she should have told him what she knew about Frank Shane, but there was also the question of Anna Collier, Frank's niece and Marion's close friend.

What would Anna say if Marion sicked this deadly looking stranger on to Frank to fight it out with each other. One of them would undoubtedly die and if Kells lived, Anna would become her bitterest enemy.

Marion sighed unhappily. Well, she had lost the chance now, but if she had her opportunity again, she was not at all sure but what she would not urge Kells to take a look at Frank Shane of Arrow and be damned to the consequences.

Chapter Four

THE SILVER DOLLAR

The day following the gun-fight and Kells's departure from Lordville, Sheriff Race Arnold returned wearily to town, and, like his horse, was covered with dust and sweat.

Villiers, the hostler, had given him a picture of events the previous day and gaps had been filled in by sundry, eager-voiced townsmen.

Arnold slumped across his desk in the office and gazed moodily across at the opposite wall with unseeing eyes.

Sooner or later, he knew, he would have to decide what he was going to do and neither alternative was good. Only recently Frank Shane had reprimanded him, mildly, it was true, for stepping out of line over one particular incident and Shane had again reminded the sheriff of his position.

It suited Frank's book to have a nice respectable front in town in the shape of the law and over and above his county wages, Arnold received payment for doing what Arrow said. It wasn't easy to keep an ailing wife and a growing family on the pittance paid out by the county to Law Enforcement

Officers and Arnold had agreed to do 'small' things for Arrow so as to earn extra money.

It was the old story. The small things grew to larger ones and if and when Arnold baulked, Shane smiled gently and reminded the sheriff of his sick wife and kids. Once, Arnold had gone for his gun, but as Frank pointed out, there were fourteen Arrow riders all ready to blast him or anyone else down, given the word.

Arnold was no more of a hero than the next man. He had no hankering to die, particularly as there would be no one left to care for his family. No, there was little alternative really, once a man had started out on this particular course, yet Arnold choked on this latest pill he had been forced to swallow. This time orders had not even come from Frank. It had been that rough-and-tumble gun-slinger, George Schillinger, who had word for Arnold to get out of town for a whole twenty-four hours, and the sheriff had known it was so that Schillinger could blast this man Kells with two-three of his sidekicks to help him.

Well, Arnold had made his play the other night and had gone as far as he had dared, farther in fact, in throwing his gun on Schillinger and the Arrow riders. What was he to do? Go back and start toeing the line again as he had done in the past, or start dishing out some law?

Arnold knew with a cold certainty, that if

it were to be the latter, not only would his family suffer in some way, but he himself would not live much longer. It would be a bushwhacking with no proof to the county officers of who had done it. There would be murmurs of road-agents and outlaws and once again Frank Shane and his Arrow riders would go scot free.

Arnold rolled and lit a smoke, his leathery face wrinkled in thought. Better by far have let this stranger Kells fight his own battles, he told himself. And yet, some good had come out of this. Kells had brilliantly out-fought Schillinger and Foley Kessel, so the story ran, and Marion had magnificently settled Luke Putnam's hash. At least two of Frank's gun-slingers would make no more trouble and George himself was not likely to stir anything up, much, for the next month.

Arnold thought of his wife, May, and the boy, Bud, and Tina and Sally, the youngest. A lump came into his throat and he pushed the thoughts and mental pictures into the background. From now on, he decided, he would play both ends against the middle. A dangerous game in all truths. He would agree with Frank on the surface and work against him underground as much as possible. Pity Lee Kells was here no more to give his help.

About five miles down the valley, in the vast bend of the Creation River, the Arrow spread was situated and here, Frank Shane, subject of Sheriff Arnold's bitter thoughts, was wrestling with his own problems.

Shane was a big man, square and chunky and with a face the colour of an old saddle blanket. His crisp, curling hair, once dark brown, was now turning grey, yet there was no suggestion even of middle age in the Arrow owner's appearance or condition. He was as strong as a lion and more than one waddy on the spread had felt the weight of Frank's arm through some peccadillo committed indiscreetly.

Frank stood on the gallery of the house, gazing out at the waving buffalo grass in the nearer meadows and putting his glance farther afield to the river and the foothills beyond where cattle grazed peacefully in large numbers. His cattle, his land, by right of might and the ability to take and hold what he claimed as his own.

His gaze shuttled back now to the other buildings; bunkhouse, corrals, stables, blacksmith shop, and settled on the slim yet shapely figure of his niece, Anna Collier.

Damn her, Shane thought, chewing savagely on his cigar. She was like a mill-stone round a man's neck. So were all women for that matter. That was why he had never married.

Three years ago, Anna had been sent west to the ranch by her parents for a vacation and only a few months after she had arrived, word was received that both her mother and father had been killed in a railroad accident.

Anna had not been able to get back for the funeral, but she had returned home to pay her respects at the graveyard and to settle up things back east. She had returned as a result of Frank's half-hearted invitation and Shane had cursed frequently after that, little dreaming that the girl would decide to make her home out here.

Yet he ought to have known. There was nothing back east to keep her there and Frank Shane was her only living relative.

Anna did not know about the change of name. That had been ten years back when the girl had been but nine years old. If she had ever noticed that her parents had referred to Uncle Frank as Frank Shards it was doubtful whether she attached any significance to it. In her younger days it had always been Uncle Frank when reference was made to her mother's brother and later on, Anna's family accepted the change from Shards to Shane without any question.

Frank had felt for a long time that Anna was a sort of restraining influence. She put a brake on a man's schemes just by the way she looked at him out of those level blue eyes. She hated cruelty and, surprisingly, would flare up whenever she caught a rider using a horse or a dogie in what she called a 'callous' manner. And when Anna Collier flew into a temper in defence of something, it was a brave man who stepped in to deal with her.

Even Frank, strangely, with all his carefully concealed brutality and contempt for most decent things, even he, always felt an odd, almost superstitious reluctance to handle his niece until she had cooled down.

And it wasn't only Frank himself. Even hard cases like Schillinger, the tall Schultz and the rest of the bunch dropped their gaze and shuffled uncomfortably when Anna Collier got mad at them.

They steered clear of the Boss's niece as much as possible, but somehow she was always around when a man least expected or wanted it. She sure got under a man's feet and Frank swore again and threw down the cigar butt.

He turned back into the house, tramping heavily upstairs and entering one of the rooms in the ranch's upper storey.

He gazed down at the figure of Schillinger lying in bed and felt a sudden wave of sadistic pleasure as though here, in his ramrod's pain and misfortune, was an antidote to the anger which had built itself inside him.

'And how does Arrow's ace gun-slinger feel to-day?' he sneered, looking down into Schillinger's glittering black eyes. 'You sure are a mess, George. Better watch out who you tangle with next time.'

'I'll be all right in a day or two, Frank,'

Schillinger gritted. He was feeling scared that Shane might throw him out now. It was something which George Schillinger could not really contemplate. He felt a part of Arrow; almost as much as Frank himself. And he had his pride too, which now had been humbled and dragged in the dust.

Shane seated himself heavily in a stout wooden chair and lit a fresh cigar, purposely blowing the smoke in Schillinger's direction. Doc Ivory had stipulated, amongst other things, no smoking and no spirits.

'You'll be laid up best part of two months if you want the truth,' Frank said with brutal honesty. 'Doc told me so himself whatever he fobbed you off with.'

Schillinger's jaw sagged so that his broken and blackened teeth showed in revolting detail. He passed a tongue over dry lips.

'Two months?' he echoed softly. 'Christ! What's goin' to happen, Frank. Who–'

Shane smiled. He was enjoying himself. His former anger had evaporated.

'I'll be gettin' someone to take your place, George. One of the boys, perhaps. I don't know which one yet. Oh, only for a time, of course, until you're on your feet again. The work's got to go on you know. We'll be moving cows north of the river pretty soon so as to make sure of that land. While we're doin' that we'll squeeze out those two damned rawhiders who are squattin' on Clayton's Strip.'

'Clayton's Strip? Yeah, but the Rust brothers is sure tough to shift, Frank–'

Shane smiled. 'Who said they weren't, George? Who said they weren't? But I don't go for folks crowdin' me and the Rust brothers is too dam' close for my likin'.

'We've taken nearly all their cows already you remember?' Shane went on complacently. 'If that don't shift 'em, maybe powder smoke will!'

'I'd like to get even with thet Kells bastard!' Schillinger gritted. 'Clean busted my arm with .45 slug. Hope to God Doc Ivory's set it proper.'

'Kells, eh?' Shane ruminated. 'Name seems kind of familiar now you mention it again. Guess I probably knew someone of that name in the old days, maybe down in the San Saba Valley. But I reckon it don't matter a lot–'

'What you goin' to do about thet interferin' bitch Marion Starr, Frank? Killed Luke she did, Ivory said. We could sure enough get her convicted an'–'

'Don't talk like a fool, George,' Shane snapped. 'There are some things that even we can't do. Why, that girl's a public heroine now, in the eyes of Lordville. She's got the whole town rootin' for her an' soon it'll be all over the county. We could never get away with it even if we wanted to. Besides which she's Anna's friend. No, George, you'd best forget anything like that else you and me are going to fall out.'

The words were quietly spoken but there was a cold menace behind them which did not fail to register with the wounded ramrod. He shivered slightly as his gaze lifted to the granite face of the Arrow owner.

Frank nodded shortly, dismissing the whole thing with that one arrogant gesture and turned and left the room.

Lee Kells had made his way unhurriedly through the heat of that afternoon until dusk had fallen, shrouding the trail and the whole of Creation Valley in its blue-grey haze.

He had slept the night at a small horse ranch near to the trail and only the following morning did he discover the loss of his gold-poke.

He cursed quietly as he searched his pockets for the fourth or fifth time, looking also in the most unlikely places; his saddle-bags, for instance; his blanket roll; his war-bag; even inside his boots. Slowly he came to the bitter conclusion that somewhere along the trail between here and Lordville, somewhere perhaps where he had left the trail to explore the country on either side, he had lost all his worldly wealth. There had been a tidy sum in that leathern poke, he reflected morosely. Gold and silver as well as greenbacks. Now he had just about sufficient money in his pants' pocket to square up with the rancher who had fed and housed him and tended his horse.

He realized the utter futility of going back to make a search even as the idea came to his mind. There were nearly twenty miles between Lee Kells and Lordville and a vast expanse of rolling country with tangled arroyos and grassy, wooded draws on either side of the trail. The poke could be hidden in grass or undergrowth in any one of a thousand, aye, a million places and might never be recovered.

It looked like the first thing he would have to do on reaching Hide City was to hire himself out again as a ranch hand as he had done so many times in the past.

Only by this method had he been able to pursue so relentlessly and steadily the trail of Frank Shards, one-time nester, and principal actor in the tragedy which had resulted in Ezra Kells' lynching.

The rancher had said Hide City was another thirty odd miles along the trail and Kells figured he could make it easily by late afternoon. He had some scraps of food in his saddle-bags, a pint bottle of whisky and a canteen of water. Beyond his horse, guns and shells and the clothes he wore, he had nothing except one remaining silver dollar.

Of all the times for a thing like this to happen, Kells thought bleakly, spurring the roan and white to a faster gait. This would probably mean another frustrating delay in checking up on whether the man he was after were indeed still in Hide City or lived near by.

Without money, there was not much you could do. A man had to eat and drink and sleep and above all care for his horse. Kells cursed again and pushed obstinately ahead for his destination, not bothering to halt, except occasionally to rest his horse.

All day he rode until by late afternoon, hungry, thirsty and tired, he rode into the county town, Hide City. There was just one silver dollar in his pants' pocket and every now and again his hand slid to it and his mind probed how best he could spend it. It wouldn't buy much. Not when he wanted a bath and a shave, a drink and a meal, a night's lodging and stabling and feed for his horse.

He saw the saloon then, across the dusty, noisy street. 'The Silver Dollar Saloon.'

Kells racked his horse at the tie-rail and stepped tiredly from the saddle, wondering whether or no this were an omen.

Hell! He hadn't much to lose by trying his luck. One spin on the wheel and it would be gone – or else multiplied considerably.

He pushed through the doors and into the lamplit interior.

This was some place, he thought. Swell

fixings, including an ornate bar mirror, a huge painting of a nude woman, and a complete lay-out for most of the various games of chance. Faro, roulette, monte and poker tables lay against the further wall. Percentage girls moved provocatively amongst the customers, some sitting on the knees of those drinking at booths or tables.

A girl, lovely underneath her heavy make-up, stood at the roulette table spinning the wheel.

He heard someone address her by name. 'Lea,' the man said. Well, that was pretty close to 'Lee,' Kells thought and for the first time that day the deadly expression left his face.

Men who had watched his entry, now relaxed and re-applied themselves to the drink and the women. One or two percentage girls eyed him speculatively, trying out their stock smiles and stock phrases.

Kells brushed them aside as though they did not exist.

The roulette girl looked up and for a brief second her eyes met Kells' gaze in an expression of deep interest – almost it seemed, recognition.

'Chips, stranger?' she said in a low, throaty voice.

'A dollar's worth,' he said, fumbling in his pocket and sensing rather than seeing the half-contemptuous glances of those at the table.

The girl had watched him as he had drawn the silver piece from his pocket, and like the others she knew this was all he had.

The chances against any chosen number coming up were considerable but Kells chose eight and put his money on it.

The wheel was spun and fascinated, eager gazes held tightly to the ball as it bounced from one slot to another and slowly, very slowly, came to rest in eight. It gave one last jump, to a low chorus of gasps and grunts, but decided to stay right where it was.

'You win, stranger,' the girl said, pushing a stack of chips over to Kells.

He looked at her, amazed somehow at his own good luck, yet doubtful and uncertain whether to push it further.

Almost imperceptibly the girl's dark head nodded. Kells was sure no one else had noticed. He was not even certain about it himself. He pushed the pile of chips across the marked-out baize table, placing them again on eight.

'*En plein?*' the croupier asked and Keels nodded tightly.

'No more bets, gentlemen,' the girl Lea called as she started the wheel spinning and, apparently carelessly, threw in the ball.

The wheel spun and slowed down. Once again the ball clicked into the 'eight' compartment.

Exclamations of surprise, chagrin and

plain envy greeted this second whirl of luck that the tall stranger had got for himself.

Kells had never been so stunned in his life, yet nibbling into his dazed mind already, was the suspicion – no the certainty – that his girl, Lea, was working a crooked wheel but, working it in his favour.

There was much excited talk going on and movement of men crowding behind the chairs at the table and, just for a moment, Kells found the girl at his side.

Her painted mouth hardly moved as she whispered, 'Cash in now, stranger. Don't push your luck further!' She was back to her place at the wheel before Kells could think up any reply. He looked at Lea and found her watching him intently and suddenly he had the idea that he had seen this girl some place else. Her head moved slightly from side to side and the croupier, now regarding Kells with a cold, unfriendly eye, suggested that the stranger might care to stake his pile, or some of it, once again, on his lucky number.

Kells smiled thinly and shook his head. 'I'll cash in now,' he said and the croupier looking him over, noting this man's powerful frame and the well-handled Colt at his right hip, merely nodded. He turned to Lea and asked. 'Where's Art?'

The girl shrugged smooth white shoulders. 'Out, I guess, Fred. You'd better get the stranger cash. Art wouldn't like us to welsh on a bet. Guess the stranger wouldn't either.'

The croupier nodded and made a rapid computation on a piece of paper. He beckoned to a houseman to fill his place and walked off to a rear door.

He returned a few minutes later with bundles of notes, neatly parcelled with rubber bands.

'One thousand dollars, mister. First time that's been done since Lucky Larry Fowler busted the bank. But that took Larry all night.'

Kells nodded absently and stuffed the bills into the pockets of his coat. He made for the bar and called for whisky and gradually the incident at the roulette table took a back seat as men crowded round to try their luck and vied with each other to place their bets on lucky eight.

Kells smelt the perfume, aware that the girl was standing next to him. A houseman had taken over the wheel and the girl was free for the moment.

'Reckon that was worth a drink, stranger?' the husky voice said and Kells smiled suddenly and said, 'Sure.'

The barkeep pushed another shot glass across the counter and Lee poured whisky from the bottle.

'Let's go some place we can talk, Lea,' he said, catching up the drinks and moving over to an empty table against the wall.

She nodded, following him through the crowd and selecting the chair next to him.

'Why did you do it, Lea?' Kells said softly 'and if it comes to that, who the heck are you, anyway? I'm near plumb certain I've seen you before and I'm not handing you out a line…'

She smiled. 'I know you're not, stranger. Reckon a girl gets to be a right smart judge of men, in my job. But you're right about having seen me before, though I didn't expect you'd recognize me or remember, straight away.

'You recollect a joint in San Antonio about two-three years ago? A place called "The Golden Angel"?'

Kells frowned, searching the recesses of his mind, trying to recollect something which, to him, was probably of little significance.

Suddenly his face cleared and the smile chased away the tightness in his jaw and the thin line of his lips.

'Say!' he grinned in sudden remembrance. '"The Golden Angel!" Yes! And – no! don't tell me! – you were Angel Frenchie or Frenchard–'

'Franchot,' she supplied, pleased that he should remember after all this time.

'Now I am just Angelea Franchot. But perhaps you don't remember that you saved me from a very nasty pawing by a Texas "gentleman" who was very drunk?

'No,' she decided. 'I guess you wouldn't remember a thing like that. But I never forgot–'

A light began to dawn in Kells' eyes as the incident, trivial enough in itself, came back to him with astonishing clarity now that he had racked his brains and set in motion the rusty cogs of memory.

'I reckon I remember now,' he told the girl; 'I can even mind the Texas "gentleman" who got you – and me – fighting mad. He finished up in the watering trough – completely sobered.'

They laughed over the incident, memory of which had unconsciously drawn them closer together. But Kells' face sobered as he returned to his original question. 'Apart from doing me a dam' good turn,' he said, 'What about the boss? This Art somebody or other?'

'Art Lucas! He's another I'd like to be shot of. That money's no more than he's squeezed out of hundreds of suckers and worse–'

'Then the wheel was rigged, Lea? You fixed it, somehow, for me to clean up? I'm not so sure, now–'

'About taking it?' Her thick black brows rose in genuine astonishment. 'Are you kidding, Lee? It's done you a good turn and given me a chance to get my own back on Lucas for some of the mean, low-down tricks he's played on me and others.

'But don't start a riot about it an' keep your mouth shut! You won't get Lea Franchot admitting the play was rigged against the

73

house. I don't wanta finish up with a knife or bullet in my back.'

Kells realised it was too late now to start worrying over the morals of the situation. If he tried to return the money the whole thing would look so fishy that suspicion would inevitably point to Lea. Like she said, the consequences of that could be a dry-gulcher's bullet or a knife stab from an alley one dark night.

Chapter Five

A FIGHT BY THE CREEK

Kells' next move was to find a place to eat, and after stabling the horse at W.O. Sellar's livery, he made for Ross House, a hotel which Lea had recommended and where he could get a drink, a good meal and also put up for the night. After a few drinks and a good-sized meal in the hotel restaurant, Kells made for the nearest barber shop for a shave and a bath...

Wherever he went he kept his ears and eyes open. Yet it was a tough chore trying to follow up this lead which had been given him months ago. He had only a sketchy description to go on; vague boyish memories of

74

how Frank Shards had appeared ten years ago. He did remember the scar on the back of the man's right hand, but it was scarcely enough to make identification immediate and positive. Quite a few men in this lawless west were scarred on faces, arms and hands from knife and bullet wounds or as a result of some accident through their work.

There had been a Fred Shards, one man had told him in answer to Kells' discreet enquiries. That had been nigh on twelve months back and this one had been a freighter. No, he had not been a particularly large man, Kells' information recollected. Rather the lean and wiry type of character.

Kells shrugged and dismissed any idea of following this up. He was certain that his memory was right in placing Frank Shards as a big, beefy man. That was the first requirement. Secondly, Kells was sure that even after all this time, that scar would still show white and clear against the brown skin of an outdoor man. Thirdly, it would have to be someone who knew and had worked in the San Saba Valley area and when Kells made casual mention of the district and in particular the Crockett spread, men shrugged. Some had heard of it, few knew it and Kells was forced to go easy on his questioning. He didn't want to become the centre of undue interest. After all, he was a stranger to Hide City anyway and a too inquisitive stranger might attract the attention of the Marshal or give warning to the man Kells sought, if indeed he were still in the district.

Lee had hardly expected to discover anything much at first. He had only hit town a few hours back, yet impatience burned in him with a steady flame.

This trail-town of Hide City with its cattle-loading pens, its railroad depot, its saloons, brothels and dance-halls, offered an endless variety of 'pleasures' and relaxation for trail-weary cowhands, but Kells wanted none of it.

He stood on the board-walk watching the play of light and shadow on men's faces, some bearded, others clean-shaven. He watched men's actions, noting the particular characteristics and frequently his glance fell to their hands as waddies, ranchers, store-keepers, drummers, business men, tramped the board-walks from one saloon to another.

He walked slowly and without definite purpose, exploring his way almost automatically until he came to the bubbling creek at the edge of town.

It was quiet here and peaceful. Giant cottonwoods and willows thinly fringed both banks of the softly murmuring creek. A half moon hung in the dark, star-spangled sky like a slice of golden cheese. A few late birds and insects chattered against the whisper of the water and the rustle of grass in the night wind.

But another sound hit Kells' ears; the soft swish of someone walking through the grass towards him. He remained where he was seated on the fallen tree, his hand resting lightly on his gun as he gazed into the dark shadows of the trees.

It was a slight figure which emerged from the darkness a few minutes later. Someone who appeared hesitant and uncertain and in that moment, Kells saw that it was a woman.

She wore a long, dark cloak with a hood and when, with a sudden movement of shapely hands, she threw back the hood, the moonlight caught her face and Kells, with a slight start recognized the lovely features of Lea Franchot.

'Lea!'

She swung round, facing towards him and then, identifying the shadowy figure astride the log, moved quickly across the moonlit glade and seated herself alongside, without preamble.

He thought she looked even more beautiful and desirable than she had done back in the saloon. Perhaps it was the mystic softening influence of the night, the moon and the stars...

He shook himself, feeling almost irritated.

'Do you usually wander about late at night, like this, Lea?'

Her reply startled him. 'I was looking for you.'

'What made you look in this direction? How was it you didn't tour the saloons?'

She smiled. 'Maybe I did, at that. I don't know. I guess I had a sorta feeling a man like you wants to be alone sometimes–'

'That why you horned in?'

She flushed and bit her full, red lower lip. She half rose to go, but Kells, bitter, frustrated and admittedly ornery at times, felt a sudden wave of remorse. He put his hand on her arm and felt a queer, pleasurable thrill as his fingers squeezed the soft, warm flesh where her cloak had fallen open.

'Don't take any notice of me, Lea,' he grunted. 'I'm just a damned ungrateful sorta cuss, I reckon. Plumb ornery too. You see, I–'

He plunged on, telling her the reason for his trip to Hide City; his long search over the years for the ringleader of the mob who had lynched his father. He hadn't intended telling her all this. Yet now he had poured out the whole story and she had listened attentively, obviously interested. Once or twice she had interjected a question or a remark.

Then: 'I'm terribly sorry, Lee. Somehow I guess I felt there was some kind of a background like that when I first saw you again. Sure as hell there was something that prompted me to give you a chance to grab a stake–'

'Thanks to you,' Kells said soberly, 'I can go right ahead, looking again, instead of

78

taking time off to earn more money punching cows at forty a month–'

'Say,' the girl put in. 'This Frank somebody or other. There's a Frank Shane as comes to Hide City every so often, trailing cows to the railroad. His brand is Arrow and his spread's located in the bend of Creation River, fifty miles or so down the trail.'

'I know,' Kells grinned. 'I've ridden in from Lordville. I heard about Arrow and its owner. Fact is I had a run-in with Arrow's ramrod, but I didn't get around to Frank. Didn't seem likely he was the man I was after, particularly as I'd been tipped off that Hide City was the place–'

'Wait a minute, Lee,' Lea said, clutching his arm eagerly. 'Maybe Hide City was the place your friend, or whoever it was, saw him in. But that don't mean he lives in town. Frank Shane comes here several times a year, Lee. Sometimes with cattle. Sometimes without. What's more, he nearly allus wears gloves even in warm weather. But I've seen him in the Silver Dollar when he's been playing or paying for drinks. That's when he takes his gloves off, and, get this, Lee, he's got a scar running the length of his right hand from knuckle to wrist.'

Kells sat very still for the space of a couple of minutes. 'It could be, Lea,' he said softly. 'It looks like I'm due to turn right around and trail back to Lordville.'

He reached into his coat pocket and drew out his makings.

'I could use a cigarette,' the girl said and Kells rolled two, lighting them from the same match.

He watched her smoky grey eyes as they gazed back at him through the match flame, and felt some of the ice melt in his veins.

'What happened back at the Silver Dollar, Lea? Did Lucas show up and cuss you about that roulette wheel?'

He spoke jokingly and was surprised to see her face harden and the eyes darken with anger. Her scarlet nails dug themselves deeply into the velvet cloak around her.

'Art sure didn't like it,' she said huskily. 'Reckon he 'most nearly slapped the skin off my shoulders–'

Kells leaned forward, suddenly, unaccountably blazing. 'You mean, he hit you, Lea? Say I've got a date right now with Art Lucas–' He broke off as the girl again clutched his arm.

'Don't, Lee,' she said quickly. 'That's the surest way of tearing up my meal ticket. A girl's got to live you know, and provided I'm nice to Art and do like he says–'

Kells said. 'You're his mistress?'

She looked almost surprised at that.

'Of course, what else, Lee? Have you ever figured what it's like for a woman in a cowtown, a trail-town or any other kind of burg, out west? A woman like myself, I mean, who can't teach kids, or learn them music or serve in a store–'

'Why, I guess I've never stopped to figure it out, Lea.' Kells said thoughtfully. 'But surely there's something else you can do if you want–'

'What? Name just one thing, Kells,' Lea said her voice sounding unutterably weary. 'Don't you think I've been into all this a hundred times before? Do you think I like being mauled and pawed by drunken cowpokes, miners and track labourers and working a crooked wheel and then finishing up a fourteen hour day by being "nice" to Art Lucas?'

Kells ground out his cigarette and rose from the log.

'No, I guess not,' he said slowly. 'I guess not.'

He was silent again for some minutes, staring sombrely at the moon-kissed creek where its silver ripples were visible between the trees.

'What about Lucas?' he asked presently. 'Way back you hinted at a knife or a bullet if he found out–'

'I said if I admitted it,' Lea corrected, rising to her feet and standing beside him. 'Oh, I guess he knew I'd been up to some shenanigans, but he couldn't prove it and I just natcherally swore that however I worked the wheel your number kept coming up.'

She laughed softly. 'I guess he didn't

believe me but it gave him some satisfaction to hit me–'

'I don't like that,' Kells snarled. 'Just say the word and–'

She leaned forward, placing one soft finger over his lips. 'I've got a job to keep, remember.'

She was in his arms, then without either of them knowing quite how it happened.

Her face was upturned to his and the full lips were too soft and red and tempting for Kells to resist.

She drew away presently, her face softened by the emotions which rode her and Kells caught a glimpse of diamonds in her eyes. Diamonds that sparkled more brightly than the paste ones she wore around the white column of her neck.

'Let me see you back, Lea,' he said, but she shook her head.

'I can find my way around this place,' she smiled, 'and take care of myself. Come in for a drink to-morrow before you leave.'

'That's a promise,' he told her...

Kells lit another cigarette, contemplating the glowing tip, as he thought back on Lea Franchot. The touch of her lips was still warm on his mouth, but the practical and objective side of Kells' nature told him that it was just another incident to be forgotten. Pleasant while it lasted, perhaps, like a dream and with no more substance than a dream.

Without his realising it, the lines of his face were already tightening and the old, bitter expression was rapidly replacing the former warmth in his grey eyes.

To-morrow he would start back for Lordville, he told himself, swinging off the log and toeing out the cigarette. And then, with startling suddenness, he half heard, half sensed the soft rustle behind him. He swung round fast, ducking instinctively and wheeling away from the violently descending gun butt held in the massive paw of a hairy-faced giant. Beside the big man, a small man crouched, clutching a stout club in his right hand.

The gun butt whistled past Kells' head as he swung away from that terrific blow, which, missing his face and head, glanced off his left shoulder.

A surge of anger blotted out the pain which shot through Lee's neck and arm as his long left arm reached out and caught the giant's shirt. Kells' fingers wrapped themselves in the coarse material as he heaved with all his might, dragging the bearded man forward, causing him to stumble and lose his balance. Then Kells' right fist drove hard to that black, hairy jaw, rocking the man back on his boot heels. It was almost a knockout blow but Kells' antagonist, somehow or other, contrived to keep his feet, his legs spread apart, his chest heaving.

Now the other one sprang forward raising the club before ever Kells had a chance to draw his gun.

Indeed, there was little opportunity to exchange shots in this close, savage fighting, as for the next few moments Lee fought desperately against his two attackers.

He landed a sickening blow into the smaller man's stomach, doubling him up, but the giant lumbered forward again preventing Kells from effecting any quick coup de grâce.

Lee took a jolting smack to the jaw, but managed to swerve clear of the descending club wielded by the smaller attacker. The man, carried forward by the impetus of that wicked, down-smashing stroke, came up against Lee as Kells, recovering, sent another pile-driving blow into the man's stomach. This time he did not recover so quickly. He folded up in two, his face turning a sickly green as he rolled on the trampled grass retching and vomiting.

But Lee had no time to spare on this one. Already the bearded giant was lunging forward again, forcing Kells to back-step. Any one of the blows from those flailing fists would have knocked Kells cold had they landed on his jaw. As it was he ducked and weaved, side-stepping most of the onslaught, taking advantage of his superior speed and agility.

Whenever an opening appeared in the

giant's guard Kells rained blows to the heart with all the strength he possessed. Both men were now breathing heavily, chests heaving, shirts and coats torn and faces sweaty and bloody.

Angered by his inability to down the man he had been ordered to attack, the bearded one rushed in again with a sudden and renewed fury.

This time, however, Kells came forward to meet the attack, taking several punishing and sickening blows to the body before stepping in and seizing his opportunity.

For a second, the giant's guard was down, his bearded chin thrust forward and Lee drove for the point of that chin with all the strength left in him.

The punch came right the way up from Lee's boots and, luckily, connected on the crucial spot.

He saw Blackbeard's eyes glaze over in the moonlight and for a moment the big man swayed, spraddle-legged. Then he fell backwards with a crash against the fallen log on which Kells had been sitting. Lee heard and almost felt the solid impact of the big fellow's head as it smashed against the tree-trunk.

He lay quite still, his breath making a rasping noise, his face white and blood-smeared. The other one, the smaller of the two, was moaning to himself like a wounded animal.

Kells stood back, dragging vast quantities

of air into his labouring lungs. Slowly he wiped sweat from hands, face and neck with his bandana and gradually the aching muscles in his arms and legs began to respond and co-ordinate with his brain.

He bent down over Blackbeard's body and went through the man's pockets, first thrusting the fallen six-gun into the waistband of his trousers.

There was a small amount of money, a clasp-knife, a leathern poke and sundry odds and ends, including a torn scrap of note-paper with a printed heading. The words said 'The Silver Dollar Saloon' and underneath in smaller characters, 'Art Lucas, Proprietor.'

Kells straightened up and gazed thoughtfully at the creek. The thing was beginning to jell, now.

These two hombres had been sicked on him by Art Lucas with orders to get back the thousand dollars. There could be no other explanation, he thought. It was unlikely that they would have done this on their own account, but – how had they known where to find him? It would be too much of a coincidence to expect that they, like Lea, earlier on, had just stumbled blindly on the glade by the tree-fringed creek.

Kells drew in his breath with a sudden thought. The answer could be that Lea herself had led them there and the story about

Lucas beating her something she had made up to add colour and realism to her story.

Yet Lee shook his head angrily at this. Lea Franchot, though she meant little or nothing to him, nor indeed had the kiss, did not seem the usual brazen and unscrupulous type of saloon girl.

Lee rolled and lit a cigarette, and watched the moon curving away to the south-west. He was inclined to hold to his first theory. Art Lucas had been angry and had dealt with Lea much as she had described and afterwards Lucas had called his thugs together and told them to find and beat up the stranger who had won a thousand dollars, and bring back the money.

Lucas might well be wealthy, but no man would sneeze at a thousand or let a stranger have it so easily, particularly when the wheel was rigged in favour of the house.

Lee felt in the pockets of his torn coat and shirt, reassuring himself that the money was still there and distributed about his body as it had been on leaving Ross House.

He smiled grimly at the two prone figures on the grass and turned his attention to the clean-shaven one who had finished puking and now cringed away as Kells' big shape loomed over him.

He offered no resistance as Lee rummaged through his pockets, fishing out a deck of greasy cards, some money, and several scraps of paper, some of which, by the printing on them, had obviously come from the Silver Dollar and probably out of Art Lucas' private room.

There was no doubt left in the mind of Lee Kells, that Art had set these two gunsels on to him in order to recover the money and at the same time give him a thorough working-over to discourage any future ideas about tangling with the owner of the Silver Dollar.

Lee grinned again. Art Lucas would be a surprised man to-morrow, when Kells showed up for his morning drink...

Chapter Six

ARROW HIRES A FOREMAN

In spite of the fact that he had returned to the hotel at a comparatively late hour the previous night and in spite of the aches and bruises on his face and body, Lee awoke early, throwing off the blankets and pulling on shirt and pants.

He withdrew the money and the spare six-gun from underneath the pillow, transferring them to the tattered and mud-stained coat. Then he crossed the room, poured water from the cracked pitcher into the bowl and sluiced hands and face.

He shaved in the same water, taking care, as far as possible, to avoid the cuts and go easily over the bruises which were now beginning to appear as purple-black blotches.

He studied his face in the mirror and considered that by and large he had not come off so badly, wondering how the two gunsels were feeling this morning if, indeed, Blackbeard were feeling anything at all. It would not surprise Kells to learn that the big man had been killed when he smashed his head against the fallen tree.

The thought, however, neither alarmed Kells nor concerned him unduly. Whatever came to his two attackers was only what such scum deserved and was usually brought on themselves. As regards any action from the Marshal, well, obviously there was nothing to point the finger at Lee Kells. Art Lucas would not admit sicking the men on to him. It would mean too many explanations and Kells doubted whether – in a town of this size, the county town at that – Art Lucas had the lawmen in his pocket. It was very unlikely.

Shortly he descended to the restaurant downstairs and consumed a large breakfast.

At eight o'clock he paid his bill and lugged his blanket-roll and carbine down to the livery.

W.O. Sellar's place was open, with a button

in charge, and Kells saddled up and lashed blanket-roll to the cantle, finally thrusting the Winchester into the off-side saddle-boot. He paid the boy, but left the pony in the stall, emerging into the sunlit street in time to witness a dazed and sleepy-eyed Hide City greet another day.

From the veranda of the hotel, Lee watched stores and saloons open up and soon riders were coming and going and men beginning to throng the side-walks bent on business or pleasure, or both.

Inside the Silver Dollar, Kells leisured his way over to the bar where a sprinkling of early customers lined the counter. Gaming tables were not occupied as yet and only one tired percentage girl was to be seen wandering idly about the room at the far end.

Kells wondered what time Lea and Art Lucas usually put in an appearance.

The barkeep, a dark-haired, sallow-complexioned man, eyed Kells uncertainly. He recognised this big fellow as the stranger who had 'cleaned' the roulette wheel early last night. He had received no specific orders, therefore he figured it was okay to serve him. In any case, the barkeep's considered opinion was that it would be unwise to refuse.

Kells drank his whisky slowly. He was in no hurry. Soon he would be on the trail back to Lordville and with more *dinero* than when he had left.

He would examine the Bend of Creation River and give the Arrow owner a looking over. Just how he would do this he had not, as yet, determined.

His eye caught sight of the shirt-sleeved figure emerging from a private door in back of the room. The man was tall and big-boned with slicked down black hair, black sweeping moustaches across a pale, sallow face.

He wore a fancy waistcoat and grey, striped pants, sufficiently tight-fitting to reveal massive leg muscles. Without a doubt, this would be Art Lucas.

Kells watched him, knowing that in a moment or two their glances would clash.

It was no more than a second later that Art Lucas' bright gaze caught and held to the tall figure at the bar. Kells saw the man's eyes flicker as though with sudden recognition. It was obvious, Lee thought, that Art had not only had his description but had also probably extracted his name from Lea Franchot.

Lucas walked slowly towards the bar. On his face was a disarming smile.

'Morning, stranger,' he greeted. 'I reckon you must be the pilgrim as nearly busted the roulette bank last night?'

'The same,' Kells admitted quietly. 'And that wasn't the only thing – I made a better job of bustin' the other two.'

'The other two?' the big man's tone was one of mild interest.

'Sure,' Kells smiled. 'The two gunnies who jumped me last night and tried to roll me for the *dinero*.' Kells was watching closely as he spoke. For a brief flash anger sparked in Art Lucas' dark brown eyes. For a moment only it was there and then gone.

'Say, that was tough,' he drawled. 'I can see now you've been in a fight. Got quite a few cuts and bruises. Know who these – er – men were?'

Kells finished his drink before replying. Then he turned with his back to the bar, leaning both elbows negligently on the counter. 'Reckon you'd know them better than I would, Lucas,' he said softly, 'only they might be a mite difficult to identify now.'

This time, Art's smile was more forced, an uneasy sort of grin, rather than the former, engaging smile.

'How so?'

Kells rolled a cigarette and lit it. He was watching points and was on his toes, but he did not figure Lucas would start anything now. Moreover, from the corner of his eye, Lee had just seen a man enter wearing a marshal's star, and make for the other end of the bar.

Kells leaned forward, his voice when he spoke carried only to the Silver Dollar proprietor.

'The big, dumb ox might well stay permanently dumb, Lucas,' he said. 'Last time

I saw him, he was spreading what brains he had over a tree-trunk. The little fella hasn't got much more than a bruised face and the belly-ache. Reckon maybe you should tread on rats,' Lee smiled. 'Maybe I will, next time, if he tries to club my head in again.'

Art passed a pink tongue over lips gone suddenly dry. He was unsure of this big stranger. Unsure, too, how much he knew and how far he was prepared to go.

As though reading his thoughts, Kells inclined his head towards the end of the bar.

'I see the Marshal's just come in, Art. You wouldn't want to make anything of this, would you?'

Lucas recovered quickly now. He laughed heartily as though the stranger had told a priceless joke. He clapped Kells on the shoulder in friendly fashion, taking care to move slowly and easily, avoiding any sudden movement.

'You're a man after my own heart, Kells,' he said, using Lee's name for the first time. 'Reckon we're both the kind who get what he goes out for, eh? Forget that little fracas last night. I'm not admitting anything, see? Let's just say it was a slight misunderstanding.'

'Reckon Blackbeard might consider it more than a misunderstanding, if he's still alive, Art,' Kells said mildly. His glance moved over to the stairs down which Lea was descending.

He raised his arm, beckoning the girl over. 'Come and have a drink, Lea,' he grinned. 'Barkeep! A drink for Miss Franchot.'

'Mr Kells and I have had a most interesting chat, Lea,' Lucas smiled as he picked up a bottle and sloshed liquor into two shot glasses. He smiled at the girl. 'A very interesting man, Mr Kells, and most capable.'

Lea said nothing. She looked as though she could use the drink which Art had poured.

Kells peeled a five-spot from one of the rolls of notes in his pockets and Art's glittering gaze held to the pile of greenbacks with the intensity of a snake watching a rabbit.

Kells was completely at his ease, as he pushed back his stetson and smiled benignly on the company. He finished his drink and gathered up the change from the barkeep.

'It's been nice meeting you folk,' he said easily. 'Maybe I'll see you again if I come back to Hide City.'

'You leaving so soon?' There was the faintest trace of regret in Art's voice.

Lee nodded, making no secret of his immediate plans. 'Going back to Lordville. Heard tell there's a man there, maybe – another rat, Art, and one I've been trailing for ten years.'

Kells's eyes were so bleak and cold and so full of murder that even Art Lucas shivered slightly, warm though the morning was.

'Hope you catch up with him, Kells.'

'I'll get him if it takes a life-time.'

There was a hushed silence following these last words which had been gritted out softly from between tightly clamped teeth.

Kells idly drew his big colt, thumbed back the hammer and spun the cylinder. He lowered the hammer gently and slid the .45 back into its oiled holster.

There was something so deadly, so sinister in that simple, everyday action, that the silence continued, stickily, uneasily for a moment longer.

It was Lucas who spoke then.

'You ever figure on a business partnership, Kells,' he said. 'You come back here and see me. Right?'

Lee's glance shuttled thoughtfully from the girl's face to Art's.

'Maybe,' he said slowly, and then added wickedly. 'Maybe I'll come back anyway just to see Lea.'

Lucas's face flushed darkly but he had his temper well in hand.

'You do that, Kells, any time,' he said.

Lee nodded, patted the girl's arm and heard her whispered, husky, good-bye, as he turned on his heel and left the Silver Dollar Saloon.

It was approaching dusk, two days later, when Kells again hit Lordville. He had taken his time but at that the hours had sped quickly enough. Lee had plenty to think about. Art Lucas for one, and Lea Franchot, who had come to him that night either to be with him or else to lead Art's two henchmen to their quarry. He was still not quite sure which it had been.

Blackbeard's body had been found just before Kells had swung out of the county town. The man was quite dead. He had been identified as Dutch Zimmerman, a hanger-on at the Silver Dollar. No one had known anything. No charges had been preferred and Kells saw no reason to go into explanations with the Marshal which might quite well result in delays, if nothing worse. Candy Stringer, the other man, had kept his mouth tightly shut, though the Marshal had observed his bruised and blackened face with more than a hint of suspicion.

But Kells had not been stopped and now, once again, he was watching Lordville awaken for its nightly activity.

He racked the pony in front of Marion Starr's restaurant, ducked under the tie-rail and moved across the board-walk to the open door.

He grinned as he saw Marion at the counter, loading trays with orders for the sprinkling of customers, and watched her face break into a warm smile of welcome.

'I'll be right with you, Lee,' she said quickly as he chose an empty table. 'I guess we didn't figure on seeing you back so soon.'

Kells rolled and lit a cigarette, waiting until Marion could come and take his order. When she crossed over to the table, he said. 'Any Arrow riders been troubling you?'

She shook her head, laughing softly. 'I'd say you threw a big enough scare into most of them. Anyway, it was always Schillinger who bothered me, not the others–' She broke off suddenly as two newcomers entered the restaurant and chose a secluded corner table. The man was big, big as Kells, and if anything heavier. The girl with him was fair-haired and blue-eyed and wore a turquoise blue dress with a bonnet to match.

'Frank Shane and his niece, Anna Collier,' Marion said as she turned back to the kitchen for Kells' supper.

Lee studied the man as best he could across the lamp-lit room. It was impossible to see, at that distance, whether or no any scar showed up on the back of his hand. But Kells had a vague, almost uneasy feeling about this Frank Shane. One moment he felt sure about him, the next, uncertain; and indecision was a trait foreign enough to Kells' make-up to cause him to feel intense irritation.

Marion came over with his meal and Lee ate in a moody silence. As he drank his coffee and rolled a cigarette, Sheriff Race Arnold came in for supper, his eye roving round the room, selecting a table and remarking the folk who were already here.

He spotted Kells almost at once, and called his name. Lee, looking up, put his glance past the sheriff to where both Frank Shane and his niece were gazing at him with a sudden, intense interest.

In a moment, the barrel-chested Arrow owner had risen and had caught Race Arnold's arm.

'If that's Lee Kells,' he boomed, 'I reckon I'd like to meet him. Figger he kinda owes that to me anyway for cripplin' my foreman.'

In a matter of seconds, Kells had leisured his way over to Frank Shane's table and was introduced by the sheriff.

Arnold presently excused himself, making for another table and Shane turned to Kells, an easy smile on his heavy face.

'So you're the jasper who shot-up George and downed Foley Kessel all in between drinks?' he grinned. 'Say, Kells, I've been wantin' to meet you.'

Anna Collier's blue eyes twinkled. 'You mustn't take too much notice of Frank,' she warned. 'He's a rough diamond, but all wool and a yard wide, and underneath that big chest he really has got a heart.'

Kells could not refrain from grinning at Frank Shane's discomfiture. There was a subtle mockery in Anna's voice, not vindictive, but sufficiently joshing to cause Shane's roan cheeks to flush dark with momentary embarrassment.

'Sit down, man,' Shane snapped, 'and have some coffee. Anna's got the tongue of a viper as you'll soon find out.'

It was all pleasantly jocular, yet Kells wondered grimly how all this would end. He had already looked for and seen the white scar on the back of Shane's hand, but was it as long and as wide as he seemed to remember from his boyhood recollections?

'–Say! I don't even reckon you're listenin', Kells!' Shane's voice cut a swathe through Lee's thoughts. He hauled up with a start.

'Thanks to you an' your quick-fire shootin', I'm short on a foreman – likely to be for a month or more and like I was saying, I'd figure you was the right size and shape for the job. What you say? We won't fight about *dinero*, if that's what's on your mind, Kells. Say a hundred a month and bonuses on trail-drives–?'

Kells was thinking hard. I'm not sure even now whether this is the man. But if I take this job, maybe I can watch him. It's no good tackling him outright. He'd probably deny the whole thing, even to having changed his name.

'Well! What do you say, Kells. Here, Anna, you try and persuade the ornery crittur. Don't look like he wants the job. Maybe the money–'

Kells shook his head. 'I wasn't thinking of the money,' he admitted, 'but maybe I had plans.'

Shane snorted like an angry bull. 'Never yet met up with any plans as couldn't be changed fast enough if the pay was right,' he grinned. 'What you say, Anna?'

The girl's blue eyes regarded Kells levelly. There was none of the china-doll prettiness about Anna Collier as she ran her gaze over Kells, sizing him up, looking at his hands for rope calluses and burns.

'I'd say he'd make a right smart foreman, Frank,' she said presently. 'If I'm not very much mistaken, Mr Kells has been a top-hand on more than one Texas spread.'

This woman had perspicacity as well as good looks, Kells thought. Undoubtedly hers was an example of beauty and brains going together.

'What I can't figure, Shane,' Lee said, 'is why you aren't gunning for me? Why we're all sitting here plumb peaceful, you offering me a job, when I cracked down on your foreman and killed one of your riders.'

Shane's big head nodded in understanding. 'Maybe I didn't make myself clear in the first place,' he explained. 'George has been gettin' a mite troublesome for quite a while now. You might say he'd got right out of hand. What's more he was takin' Luke Putnam and Foley Kessel with him. Reckon you may not have heard, Arrow's gettin' a right smart bad name hereabouts most due to those three jaspers.

'Well now, George is laid up and I ain't figurin' on lettin' him ramrod the spread again, anyway, and with Kessel and Putnam gone I can use a few more riders, 'specially a good foreman.'

'What Frank's trying to say,' Anna put in suddenly, 'is that Arrow doesn't hold with murders and killings and bushwhackings. That was a dastardly thing Schillinger tried to do to you, Mr Kells. We heard all about it and if George hadn't been with Arrow for so long, well, I reckon Frank would turn him over to Race Arnold as soon as he is better. As it is—'

'As it is,' Shane interrupted, 'I'm not worryin' overmuch about George and certainly we ain't sheddin' crocodile tears over his two cronies. Point is, are you goin' to take this job or not?'

Kells was aware of Anna Collier's steady blue eyes watching him. He became aware, also, of a sudden commotion going on in back of him, near the restaurant door. Faces turned and heads craned as the screen door burst violently inwards and a man lurched drunkenly forward, peering intently at the faces of the diners, whilst he waved a long barrelled colt in his right hand. He hiccuped and belched violently and when he spoke his voice was slurred with too much liquor.

'W-where's thet bustard of a no-good, stinkin' sheriff? Ah!' he grunted suddenly as his bleary gaze fastened on the grey face of Sheriff Arnold at a table some few yards away.

The man stood there, legs wide apart to support his swaying body, but the gun, now levelled and cocked was paradoxically held with frightening steadiness. The gaping muzzle pointed straight at Race Arnold's chest.

The room, over half full of people was frozen stiff into a silent and rigid tableau. No man's hand dare move to his gun, least of all Race Arnold's, for fear of setting a match to the powder keg of this man's drunken madness.

Whether he had a legitimate grievance against the sheriff or whether this was merely the crazy effect of two much red-eye, no one knew. It was not important anyway. Sufficient that in a second or two murder might well be done with no hand lifted to stop it.

The poor drunken fool, Kells thought, would probably have no recollection of what he had done by the next morning – if he were allowed to live that long! Lee considered he would mostly likely be set upon afterwards by the crowd and strung up there and then, without any formalities.

It was then that Shane and Anna Collier were jolted out of their trance-like mood by the sudden lightning movement of Lee Kells. No one really saw it happen, so intent were they, gazing with an awful fascination at the mouthing figure with the gun pointed at the sheriff.

Of a sudden, Kells' big colt filled its owner's right hand. The hammer came back and down, and the gun crashed out, echoing round the narrow confines of the room. Powder-smoke drifted lazily from Lee's gun and the acrid smell became a sharp tang in the nostrils of those at the nearby tables.

The man still stood just inside the doorway, but now he was staring stupidly at the bloody fingers of his right hand. The six-gun lay on the floor where Kells' bullet had sent it with one fast and amazingly accurate shot.

It had slid almost to Arnold's feet and with commendable speed and presence of mind, the sheriff stooped and scooped it up with his right hand.

A long, shuddering sigh seemed to leave everybody in the room. A sigh of relief, of tension suddenly eased. Glances shuttled from the drunk, who was now rapidly sobering, to the grim-faced stranger who had so coolly drawn and sent a snapshot with such startling and unnerving accuracy.

In a moment or two, Race Arnold, with the help of a man nearby, had handcuffed the now dazed drunk and was shoving him violently through the doors. Other folk were clapping Kells on the back as he replaced the gun in its holster.

In less than ten minutes the restaurant was restored to order and conversation was buzzing, loaded with excited speculation.

'What were we saying?' Kells said. 'Oh, yes. About that job. Well, Shane, you've done hired yourself a foreman.'

Chapter Seven

ARROW

The Arrow spread, nestling in the big bend of Creation River was a sight for sore eyes.

As soon as Kells saw it he felt a strange, unnatural surge of envy against Frank Shane, the man who had built this up.

How had it been built? Kells wondered, as he sat his horse, gazing at the neat and workmanlike buildings. Had Shane driven Crockett mavericks up from the San Saba Valley nigh on ten years ago? Was that how Arrow had been born? Or was Frank Shane really Frank Shane and not Frank Shards? A big and hearty, but perhaps, ruthless cattle owner, who'd seized virgin land and had held it against all comers and had dotted it with cows and beef critturs legitimately bought.

Kells' glance dragged itself away from the long, double-storied ranch house with its gallery and shading cotton-wood trees. He took in the trim bunkhouse, store and grain sheds, corrals and stables, blacksmith shop, windmill and a dozen other such visible signs of a big, well-run spread.

He looked now at the man and the girl in the buggy who had reined in at the ranch yard as Shane turned to Kells with something of justifiable pride on his face. It was there also in the girl's blue eyes.

'There she is,' Shane grunted unable to keep a shade of boastfulness from his voice. 'What you think, Kells?'

Lee put a hand on his mount's neck, stroking the sleek coat while his gaze went back over the panorama behind the home ranch.

'Swell,' he said at last. 'Reckon just about as nice a layout as a man could wish for.'

Shane flushed with pleasure. 'That's a mighty nice compliment, Kells. Glad you like it? Let's go an' meet the boys. You stop off at the house, Anna.'

The girl nodded as both of them descended from the buggy.

'I'll go fix some coffee for you both,' she called.

'No, we'll—' but before Shane could stop her she was on to the gallery of the ranch house.

Lee figured Shane was about to point out

that a foreman ate and slept in the bunkhouse, but neither of the men pursued the subject as they walked over towards the bunkhouse.

Last night, Kells, Frank Shane and Anna had remained over in town and this morning had got away to an early start, heading back to Arrow. It was now about ten o'clock in the forenoon and the strong sun seemed to permeate everything around with its warm, golden light, so that the greens and browns and blues of the landscape each appeared as though mixed with gold.

Most of the hands were about the place, as for some weeks past they had been gathering a herd to drive to Hide City. There were several thousand steers in the holding grounds a scant mile away so that apart from a couple or so line-riders, the men were taking a much needed rest.

One or two sat atop pole corrals. One man squatted on the steps of the bunkhouse, mending a bridle.

'Boys, I want you to meet your new foreman,' Shane said.

He looked unusually big and aggressive in the strong sunlight as though defying any man to question his right of authority or his choice in this particular case.

Kells, who had had this kind of experience in the past understood the difficulties confronting a new foreman. Separately, as a rule, the men were easy to handle and generally friendly. Together, in a bunch, they seemed to become imbued with a sharp malice, the herd instinct being a strong and ugly thing underneath the outward veneer of cool, near-hostility.

'This is Lee Kells, boys,' Shane rumbled. 'Kells meet Phil Dukes–' Lee nodded at the man who had ridden in to Lordville with Schillinger's challenge.

'–Rayner Lusgow, over there on the fence. Flip Denkern, Sol Schultz, Eddie Hindel – he's the thin hairpin one – Zip Cantrell, he's *segundo*. That's Charlie Heyman over to the blacksmith shop, and Cal Beston fetchin' water from the pump. Who's out ridin', Zip?' Shane asked the *segundo*. 'Bill Yerby and Bandy–?'

Zip Cantrell nodded though his pale, slate-coloured eyes were fixed on Kells. 'Bandy, Slim and Bill are out. Last one's over to the north-west line-cabin.'

Shane nodded. 'That's the lot then, 'cept for Curly in the cook-shack. You'll see him presently.'

Kells nodded. He thought he had rarely seen such a tough, hard-case crew as this. It would not be long before he was called upon to demonstrate his knowledge and ability. Somehow, these men would provoke and goad him, Kells knew, building up to a situation where he would be left out on a limb. Then the men would watch with cold malice while he extricated himself from the position into which they had jockeyed him. Lee smiled grimly, and there were one or two in that bunch who saw the rawhide toughness of this stranger reflected in the frigid eyes and the bleak, flat-planed face.

'We gotta take our orders from this – gent?' It was Zip Cantrell who spoke and whilst he kept his voice flat and bereft of emotion, there was a faintly discernible quality, almost contempt, about his utterance – a marked pause before he accentuated the last word of his question.

Shane nodded brusquely. It was difficult to determine whether he had read any hostility in Zip's tone and remark.

'You show Lee, here, the lay-out, Zip, and put him wise to how we run things.'

'Sure, Boss, an' while you're here, what we goin' to do 'bout breakin' in that steel-dust? She shore don't take kindly to any of us on her back.' Zip's gaze, bright with a malevolent humour all his own, shifted to Kells' face. ''Course if we had a top-hand rider – now mebbe mister Kells, here, kin ride a half-broke cayuse. Reckon he must've had plen'y experience else why would he be takin' over George's job?'

Zip Cantrell, for all the malice in his words, had nevertheless contrived to shade the tone of his voice to a certain degree of bland innocence. Cantrell was the born heckler; a man who could cause trouble by the very nuance in his words and expression. Yet there was not enough of the open insult for a man to throw down with his gun or pitch into the *segundo* with his fists.

Kells thought sombrely. Here it is and sooner than I expected.

Shane turned to Zip and his glance shuttled to the face of his new foreman.

'Guess it's up to Lee, Zip,' he said. 'If he feels like helpin' you with the steel-dust.'

Again the words were seemingly innocent, yet Kells found himself wondering whether or not Frank Shane too was ganging up with his men against him...

'She's saddled already,' Zip said. 'Been tryin' to gentle her me own self but got throwed fer me pains. Take a right smart top-hand to stay atop that cayuse.'

There it was! There was the challenge.

All eyes were now fixed on Kells and, as though the tenseness had been sensed from a distance, both Charlie Heyman and Cal Beston were now walking slowly towards the group.

'I'll try the steel-dust,' Kells said quietly, 'and form my own judgment. If she's a killer right through, it's a waste of money to keep her and plumb crazy to risk a good rider's life or limbs.'

There was a flicker of surprise in some of

109

the men's eyes; not because Kells had accepted the challenge – he had been forced to do that or quit – but in the manner of his acceptance. He was not going to be dictated to and he was a man, apparently, who was quite prepared to make his own rules and back his own judgment. Kells' stock went up a couple of notches in the opinions of Phil Dukes and Ray Lusgow...

Some of the hands were already walking towards a big corral attached to which was a small pen just large enough to hold a standing horse.

Shane said, 'You don't haveta ride that crittur, Kells. I'll warn you it's as mean as hell. No one's topped her for more'n five seconds an' we've had two busted arms apart from sprains and such like.'

'Thanks,' Kells said and walked with long, easy strides to the corral, where the hands were already clambering atop the pole fence and Zip Cantrell was motioning Kells towards the small pen.

Lee unbuckled his gun-belt and looped it over the top rail, climbing over to join the *segundo*. He had his first good view of the mare, a beautiful-looking creature with a coat like shining gun-metal. But she had a mean eye, all right, and a little blood and foam flecked her dilated nostrils.

Kells wondered who would come out on top in this fight, but he knew there was no drawing back. This was the Arrow crew's method of testing an unknown man and even though Zip Cantrell looked ugly enough to want Lee to be maimed or killed, the crew as a whole were probably quite sincere in their belief that Kells ought to do this thing as a matter of course. It was part of his job if he were going to rod the Arrow spread.

Kells was scarcely in leather before Cantrell slipped the sliding gate of the pen and whacked the steel-dust across the rump.

The animal, seeing freedom ahead and intent on throwing the rider on its back, streaked out from the pen into the main corral with the speed of a flying arrow.

Kells grabbed the reins as he was almost flung from his seat by the sudden, violent motion as a result of Cantrell's underhand action.

Even as Lee fought desperately to retain his seat and find the swinging stirrups with his boots, he resolved to see Zip Cantrell squared for this day's work sometime in the near future.

Lee hauled on the reins with such savage strength that the steel-dust found herself fighting more wildly than ever before. But only just in time Kells found the stirrups as out in the middle of the corral, the mare arched her back, flung her head down between her fore-feet and bucked her hind quarters with wild abandon.

Lee was flung forwards and backwards in the saddle and each time the steel-dust's hoofs landed, Lee was jolted with a bone-shattering force.

One or two of the Arrow men were already shouting their encouragement to Kells and Ray Lusgow sat with a huge silver timepiece in his hand.

'The sonofagun's stayed on eight seconds,' Lusgow grunted with a sly grin at Cantrell.

But Kells was unaware of anything outside the immediate business in hand.

The mare sun-fished and jumped with even greater force than before and Lee felt blood trickling down his nose, and tasted the sweet saltness of sweat and blood on his lips.

Once before he had ridden a horse like this one but, if anything, it had been worse. A killer with a killer's heart and although he had kept his seat he had known it would never be any good, nor would it ever be properly gentled. Any inexperienced rider, trying it out in all innocence, would probably have been thrown and possibly killed. Kells had shot the beast strictly against orders. That decision had cost him his job. Now he would do the same thing all over again if he felt there was no chance of breaking this half-wild steel-dust.

How long he had been in leather before he began to notice the changing tactics of the mare, Kells had no idea.

His body ached in every bone and nerve and muscle. The knuckles of his leather-brown hands showed white, tugging at the reins. His eyes were slitted against the swirling dust and his face was streaked with blood and dirt. But suddenly he became aware that the mare had slowed in her antics. She had tried the whole box of tricks to unseat this man, and had failed.

He felt her trembling and risked letting go the reins with one hand to stroke the foam and sweat stained arching neck.

He spoke to her in a low, soothing voice, leaning forwards so that his words would catch the nervously twitching ears, even as his hand continued to stroke the neck from poll down to withers.

He began walking her now, gently touching the streaming flanks with his spurs. Getting her used to the sound of his voice, the feel of his hands on the reins and the gently goading touch of the spurs...

'Five minutes, twen'y-eight seconds,' Ray Lusgow shouted. 'By Jiminy ef thet ain't ridin', then I ain't never seen any.'

Kells dismounted slowly, striving to control the shaking in his limbs and the heaving of his chest. Sweat covered his face and hands and the reins were wet as he trailed them over the steel-dust's head, leading her back to the corral fence. He did not attempt

113

to put the mare back in the small pen, but left her in the main corral, reins hitched to the top rail.

He was slowly beginning to recover his breath and now, as he approached the hands he carefully wiped sweat and blood from his face with his bandana.

'Good work, Kells,' Frank Shane said with genuine admiration in his voice. 'Reckon there ain't any doubt now, whether you can rod this spread.'

'You can say that again,' Phil Dukes murmured and several others grunted their agreement with the sentiments so expressed.

'Don't figure she wants killing,' Kells told Shane. 'Reckon maybe a few more lessons with saddle and bridle and she'll be gentled properly.'

Shane nodded. 'You want to wash up, Kells, there's a pump in back of the bunkhouse. Come over to the house when you're ready.'

Lee moved past the group of men until he came level with Zip Cantrell. He eyed him for a few moments, noting the naked dislike in the pale eyes, which Cantrell no longer troubled to camouflage.

'One of these days, Zip,' Lee said mildly, 'I'll be calling your hand.'

He turned then towards the bunkhouse, conscious of the speculative glances that followed him.

'Frank wants me to show you some of the range, Lee.'

Kells had just emerged from the bunk-house after a sound night's sleep. This morning, though his body ached somewhat, he felt remarkably refreshed. It was early as yet, and Lee was surprised to see Anna Collier, already dressed for riding.

'Mornin', Miss Anna,' he greeted. 'Frank tell you to show me the range?' Kells' question was edge with a mild surprise.

Anna Collier laughed. 'Well perhaps he didn't say that exactly,' she admitted with fresh candour. 'You see, I told Frank I wanted to ride this morning and that it would be a good way of killing two birds if I took you along and showed you some of our range.'

Kells grinned and pushed back his hat. 'Reckon I'll be glad to ride with you, Miss Collier. You've had breakfast?'

The fair hair glinted in the sun as she nodded and adjusted the white, low-crowned stetson. 'My horse is all ready in the yard. I'll wait while you saddle your paint.'

Lee nodded and touched his hat, turning on his heel towards the corrals. In less than five minutes he was riding Red around to the front of the house. Anna was already astride a sorrel, her divided skirt serving well in place of pants or breeches.

They rode for some while in silence. An easy unembarrassed kind of silence that is usually only found between two kindred sprits. The morning was warm, but not too hot and for a little while the horses had their heads. Then they slowed down to a walk.

'How do you feel after riding the steel-dust, Lee? That was a wonderful piece of bronc-busting.'

Kells smiled and the girl again noticed how the bleakness left this man's face when his thoughts were forced outwards as it were, away from whatever bitter resolves he clung to so desperately.

'Nothing more than a few aches and bruises,' he replied. 'That horse wasn't so mean right through I guess—'

'They're like humans, many of them,' the girl cut in. 'Even the worst are not often bad right through, you know.'

He shot her a swift glance, but her gaze was straight ahead. Had there been any double meaning in the remark? Had she any idea that he was here for a purpose? The purpose of discovering whether Frank Shane were indeed the man he had been trailing?

Kells didn't think so, but he could not be sure. Neither was he any nearer to discovering the truth about Frank. Yesterday he had had the opportunity of seeing the scar on Shane's hand at closer quarters, had even questioned Frank about it, casually. And

Shane had just as casually dismissed it with a brief explanation.

It had been done by a branding iron, two-three years back, he had said. That was all the explanation, yet Kells had found Shane's eyes on him once or twice as though in puzzled speculation.

'How many cattle does Arrow run – Anna?' The less formal mode of address came more easily to both of them, even though Kells was, strictly speaking, an employee.

Anna frowned in silent concentration. Surprisingly for a fair, blue-eyed girl, she had thick dark brows and black lashes, only enhancing rather than detracting from her beauty.

'I'd say about eight-ten thousand head,' she said presently. 'I don't even know whether Frank's tallied them all this year. We've cut out about two thousand for a trail-herd.'

'They're for Hide City are they?'

She nodded. 'Yes. After that maybe Frank'll want a complete round-up; gather in all the mavericks and new calves for branding and earmarking.'

'Reckon you know something about cattle and running a ranch,' Kells said, putting his gaze to the cattle-dotted rangeland.

Anna smiled. 'A bit, I guess. I came out here several times as a schoolgirl before my parents died. I was here when they were killed, back east in a railroad accident.

Before I went home, Frank kind of offered me a home here. I had no ties back east then; few friends. I was glad to accept – and her I am, though more than once I've suspected Frank has wished he never asked me to live here.'

'Doesn't he like having women about the place?'

'I guess he doesn't think a lot of women, though I'm not altogether sure it's just that. Sometimes I feel – oh, I don't know how to put it into words or why I should be talking to you like this.'

'Go on, Anna.' Kells wanted to find out as much as he could about Frank Shane. He was desperately interested, but he kept his voice at its normal, casual pitch.

'Sometimes I think,' the girl went on, 'that I put a crimp in his plans; that he can't do what he would like to with me around. You see, Lee, he doesn't mind cruelty for one thing. He'd think nothing of beating that steel-dust to death, for instance, and I'm sure he gets a kind of – well sadistic satisfaction out of hurting people. I guess he wouldn't have minded much if you had been thrown from that mare and crippled – even though he knows you're a top-hand and is as pleased as punch that he picked you out himself. That alone bolsters up his ego. He loves proving that he's right and that he knows people and animals.'

118

'Where did he come from – originally, I mean?'

'Oh, I don't know, Lee. He was out here long before I was old enough to take much interest in such things. I guess he's moved around Texas some in the last ten-fifteen years. We never heard from him for a long time; not until he had settled down here in the Bend of Creation...'

It was noon when they halted at a creek that tumbled down from the foot-hills to the north-west and picketing the horses partook of saddle rations.

Anna pointed with a long, shapely hand to the foot-hills.

'Over there, just this side of the hills is our north-western boundary. We usually have a rider at the line-cabin, watching that the cattle don't stray too far or break their necks in the ravines and dry gulches.'

Kells nodded. 'I think maybe I'll ride over that way before the week's out, relieve the rider there and have a look-see round that part of the range.'

Chapter Eight

THE MISSING PIECE

Frank Shane sat at his desk in the small room that led off from the ranch's main living-room.

Leather chairs were strewn with such odds and ends as bridles, broken straps, frayed ropes and the like. On the floor against the wall were a couple of Walker saddles the worse for wear. It was more like a junk-room than an office, but miscellaneous equipment had collected so gradually over such a long period of time, that neither Shane nor his hands noticed any untidiness. Indeed, if the place had been cleared up, Shane no doubt would have wondered at the bareness of the room.

Not that the hands were admitted here as a rule. Only George Schillinger and at times, Zip Cantrell. Now, with Schillinger upstairs with a busted arm it was the *segundo* who sat facing the Arrow owner, perched on the arm of a leather chair and smoking a quirly.

Shane moved papers on his desk, consulted a tally book for a moment, then closed it with a snap, selecting a cigar and lighting it.

He leaned back in the swivel chair, studying Cantrell through eyes half-closed against the clouds of blue smoke.

'You ever met this man Kells before, Zip? Or ever heard of him?'

'Not that I recollect, Boss,' the *segundo* said. 'Why?'

'Only that you seem to have taken a rooted dislike to him and I've been wondering why. It was hardly a fair test giving him that mare to ride.'

'He came out of that all right, didn't he?' Zip countered.

Shane nodded. 'Sure, but through no fault of yours. I saw you whack the steel-dust across the rump. Luckily for Kells he's a born horseman if ever I saw one. That ain't the first time he sat a half-busted bronc.'

'I guess I jest nacherally don't take to thet kinda hombre, anyway, Boss. He's too all-fired sure of himself.'

'With good reason!'

Cantrell ignored the interruption.

''Sides which, he downed George, didn't he, an' killed Foley an' Luke, or air you forgettin' that?'

'I ain't forgettin' it, Zip,' Frank Shane said, 'but since when did you start feeling sorry for other Arrow riders when they run into trouble? I don't recollect you shed tears when Spud Murphy got shot when we took those steers off Williams. Nor Pengelly, when he was smashed to a pulp.'

'All right, Boss. So I ain't over concerned about Kessel an' Putnam. But they were both pretty slick with their shootin' irons an' this jasper was already facin' George who never was no laggard with a hawg-laig.'

Cantrell leaned forwards across the desk. 'I'd say to watch this pilgrim Kells, boss. He's a sight too handy with horses and guns to be safe around here. 'Specially if you got any plans.'

Shane appeared to ignore the insinuation, yet his next remark showed that he was well aware of what was in Zip Cantrell's mind.

'How are the Rust boys reacting to our special brand of treatment, Zip?'

Cantrell's face creased into an evil grin.

'Reckon we've whittled their herd down to 'bout thirty-forty head. Oh, sure, they put up a beef every time they see an Arrow rider, but they ain't got a shred of proof. Even if they had it wouldn't matter, I reckon. Race Arnold wouldn't never–'

Shane waved a hand to cut short the *segundo's* speculations.

'Better make arrangements to "move" the rest of their cows off Clayton's Strip and on to Arrow range within the next week, Zip. We'll blot the brands and get rid of the cows over the border. Meanwhile we'll have the Hide City trail-herd to attend to.'

Cantrell nodded. 'What about Kells? What

you figger for him to do?'

'He's been talkin' about ridin' out to the north-west line cabin. Bill Yerby's been there nigh on a week, anyway, so it's time he was relieved. That'll leave you several days clear to smoke out those damned rawhiders – the Rust brothers.'

Cantrell grinned. It would be a pleasure, he assured his boss. Especially if they resisted...

The Arrow owner did not move from his desk, after Cantrell had left, except to light the lamp.

His mind pondered the problem which had nagged at him for the past few days. Lee Kells!

For a long time now, almost a week at any rate, Shane had felt that the name had a familiar ring.

Over the past few days he had racked his brains, was still racking them, for something to give him a lead. He felt sure there was something, if only he could think of it, and he had an uneasy feeling that this thing was important.

In the first instance he had seen Kells in Lordville and, recognising his qualities, had made up his mind immediately. Kells was the one to fill the boots of the man who now lay groggy upstairs with a busted arm.

For a long time George had been getting a mite high-handed and this was as good an

123

excuse as any to take him down a peg or two. Furthermore, Arrow needed good gunmen to protect its far-spreading herds. It needed men who could, and would, shoot straight whether against outlaw rustlers from the badlands in the north-west hills, or encroaching nesters, like these damned Rust brothers. Maybe they had a right to Clayton's Strip, but what the hell? Shoestring outfits such as theirs could not be allowed to interfere with the expansion of the biggest spread in the territory. And once Clayton's Strip was absorbed Arrow cows could move more easily across the river and extend farther north and east.

For a few moments, Frank Shane allowed himself the rare pleasure of savouring these thoughts concerning the future. Then his mind switched back again to Kells for the thousandth time. He began thinking back along the years and suddenly it was as though a switch clicked in his brain, flooding the dark recesses of his memory with illumination.

The San Saba Valley! There had been a nester there, he now remembered called Kells. What in hell had been the old buzzard's name? Ezra! That was it! But Ezra Kells had been an oldish man then and that had been, why, ten years back or more. Besides which – Shane remembered things more clearly now – they had strung up the old fool. Hadn't

Frank himself talked those other two-bit nesters into framing Ezra Kells so that he wouldn't blab to the Crockett Spread about how it was intended to star their herds with Crockett beef?

Frank Shane's face darkened with the very concentration of his thoughts. A pulse beat in his heavy cheek. He was unaware that he was sweating as he kept turning over these past events in his mind.

He remembered suddenly that Ezra Kells had had a son. Only a button, it was true. A kid of, say, ten or eleven years, and in the excitement and urgency of the hanging, little, if any, thought had been left for the boy. It was not until afterwards that Shane and the other nesters had returned to old Ezra's cabin only to find the place deserted and the gun gone from the rack and the sorry-looking crow-bait gone from the tin-roofed stable.

What in hell had been that kid's name? How had old Ezra Kells named him?

Then, with a sickening sensation, Frank bethought himself of the connection.

The Kells had been Southerners and vaguely Shane had connected this at the back of his mind with the boy. He had been named after Robert E Lee, Commander-in-chief of the Confederate Army.

Lee Kells was the son of the man he, Frank, had lynched! It couldn't be just coincidence. The name fitted. The age fitted and now another thought came to disturb Shane's already hard-working brain.

If Lee Kells were indeed old Ezra's son, then it was a sure bet he had come to Creation River for one thing. Lee Kells was looking for Frank Shards.

Whether nor he knew that Shards and Shane were one and the same man, Frank couldn't determine at the moment. But it certainly looked as though, even if Kells were not sure, then at least he was suspicious. Else why tie up with Arrow, when according to folks in Lordville, the stranger had headed out for Hide City?

But Kells had returned and at the time of returning to Lordville had met Frank and Anna in Marion Starr's restaurant.

Now Frank Shane was conscious of the sweat running down his face and neck. He used his bandana with a hand that for all its size and muscular strength, shook a little.

He went back in his mind over all the points he had thought about, checking on each link, testing it, so as to make sure there could be no mistake.

The odds were heavy against any mistake, he told himself, or any coincidence. The whole thing jibed too neatly.

Lee Kells, the son of Ezra Kells, had to be out of the way before he got on to the fact that it was Frank Shane owner of Arrow and Kells' present employer, who was the man he had been after all these years.

Shane re-lit the cigar, which he observed had long since gone out. His brain was beginning to work more smoothly now, like a well-oiled machine.

So Kells wanted to visit the northern line-cabin, did he? And Zip Cantrell hated his guts anyway.

Frank Shane began to laugh softly to himself. It was a horrible and spine-chilling sort of sound...

Anna Collier stood with her back pressed hard against the wall of the ranch house, her hands, too, flat against the boards, her whole body rigid with shock and fear.

Only a few feet along the gallery was the south-west corner of the house and beyond that, in front of the door, men's voices muttered low. Occasionally a boot scraped or a shifting chair leg shattered the tense silence of the night.

The girl's breasts rose sharply underneath the silk shirt blouse as she strove to master her agitation and quiet the pounding of her heart. She felt sure the noise of that pulsing would be heard by Frank and Zip Cantrell. She was afraid to move, terrified that her boots would squeak or scrape on the gallery floor. Now, it was as though she was literally rooted to the spot.

She had heard enough, but she dare not

move. Yet, if she stayed there any longer it was quite within the bounds of possibility that either Frank or Zip would walk along the front veranda and catch a glimpse of that white shirt in the dark shadows of the gallery.

Frank had told the *segundo* what he'd found out. Or rather what he had figured out.

Lee Kells was the son of a nester whom Frank had run into years back in the San Saba Valley. He had gone into no more detail than was necessary, therefore, Anna Collier had no way of knowing what was truth and what was falsehood.

Zip had asked few questions. His concern was not with the past but with the present and for some reason Zip hated Lee Kells as much as Frank feared him. It was, perhaps, one of those cases of fire and water, when two personalities met, and clashed, and for no known reason an antipathy was set up which grew until it reached its climax in stark physical conflict.

Be that as it may, both Zip and Frank were in unison over this, even though for different reasons. And if Zip were ready to leave straight away – Anna shuddered and strained her ears as once more the voices came softly to her through the darkness.

'You'll have to watch out, Zip, if you're goin' to get the jump on Lee Kells. We've already seen what he can do, in a small way, and I've seen him draw a gun. I tell you,

Zip, he's damned fast.'

Cantrell smiled into the night.

'I'll fix that bustard, don't worry. And I ain't aimin' on takin' fool chances, neither. Reckon by the time I'm finished et'll sure look like a bunch of outlaws has jumped the place, shot the line-rider and took off with a few cows.'

Frank said, 'When you figure to start?'

Cantrell thought a moment. 'We's fixin' to finish up at Clayton's Strip to-night, Boss. Reckon et's jest as well to get thet chore done. To-morrow I'll hit the hay for a few hours an' ride out after supper.'

There was no more information for Anna to obtain and so, under cover of the now slightly raised voices, she tiptoed back along the gallery and round the back of the house until she found the rear door.

She met no one on her way through the hall and upstairs and wrenching open the door of her room with a sob, half relief, half horror, she flung herself on to the bed, crying quietly, her head buried in the pillows...

All that day Kells rode the north-western section of Arrow range. Rough, broken country, which he explored as a matter of routine.

He made a dry camp that night, eating saddle rations and using canteen water to boil the coffee over a cheerful fire.

At dawn he rebuilt the dead fire and used

the last of his water for a breakfast cup of coffee. He had oriented himself sufficiently to know that by striking steadily westwards, he would hit the creek where he and Anna had nooned five-six days ago and as he rode he felt the relief which this day and night on the open range had afforded him away from the close confining atmosphere of the Arrow bunkhouse with its assorted mixture of riders. Some, Kells found decent enough, like Phil Dukes, Rayner Lusgow and even Sol Schultz. Others, however, were still hostile enough to make things uncomfortable generally, even though they masked their antipathy more effectively than did Zip Cantrell.

The *segundo* went to no pains to hide his dislike of Lee Kells. Apart from an instinctive animosity towards the new foreman was the obvious resentment that an outsider should be brought in to rod the spread. Not only an outsider, but a man who had killed one of the hands and had gone mighty close to putting paid to George Schillinger. This bunch of men at Arrow was not the usual bunkhouse crowd like Kells had spent time with in his past jobs.

He knew now, without any doubt, after having lived with them for a week, that most of them were hired mainly for their guns and not a few were out-and-out killers.

Schillinger himself was one, for instance, though he could cause little trouble at the moment. Zip, of course, was another such breed who would kill a man as cheerfully as swatting a fly, and so were Flip Denkern and Cal Beston.

Lee speculated on the one Arrow rider whose acquaintance he had not yet made, Bill Yerby, as he nooned at the creek some way north of where he and Anna had previously stopped.

Kells stripped the paint, put him on a long picket line and built a small fire, more for the sake of its companionship than because he needed hot grub.

Now that the fire was going, however, he placed the battered coffee-pot on the hot coals, lit a cigarette and contemplated the future with a moody kind of gloom that even the bright noon sunshine could not dispel.

He thought of the lovely Anna Collier of whom he had seen quite a deal this last week. He thought of Marion Starr with fear and grief in back of her eyes and a face and figure that would turn most men's gaze as they passed by. And for no reason at all, Kells suddenly thought of Lea Franchot, the girl who had staked him. The girl who had offered herself in the moonlight, yet surprisingly with no hint of the wanton and none of the usual saloon girl's stock-in-trade tricks. Kells grinned sardonically. That was probably the first time Lea Franchot had received no more than a kiss...

Lee drank his coffee and presently kicked out the fire and saddled his horse. It would take him best part of the afternoon to reach the line-shack, more, if he didn't get the hell out of here quickly.

His thoughts switched to the biggest problem of all, as he rode steadily north-westwards. Frank Shane! He was almost sure now; yet Kells hesitated to jump Frank and tackle him outright with the accusation. If Shane denied everything, denied ever having been in the San Saba Valley and even backed it up with some kind of 'proof' what then could Kells do, short of murdering the man in cold blood? Yet there must be some way, he thought, to clinch the thing – prove that Shane was the Frank Shards of ten years ago and then settle with him once and for all.

The sun was dipping away to the western hills when Kells, threading a way through a bunch of grazing cattle, came upon the north-western line-cabin.

A man stood in the open doorway, a rifle in the crook of his arm.

'You Bill Yerby?' Kells called as he dismounted and trailed the paint's reins.

'I'm Yerby,' the man said. 'Who are you?'

Kells rolled two cigarettes, lit them and handed one to the burly, balding man in the doorway.

He gave him the news, all of it, briefly describing the gunfight in Lordville and the succeeding events up until the tine he had been offered Schillinger's job.

'So George has got himself a busted arm?' There was the hint of laughter in Yerby's blue eyes as he carefully put down the gun, leaning it against the cabin wall.

'Shake, Kells,' he said. 'I guess I'm right pleased to meet up with a hombre who's put some salt on George's tail. How did Zip Cantrell take it?'

Kells smiled thinly 'Seems the *segundo* loves me just about as much as Schillinger does.' Kells told Yerby about riding the steel-dust and Zip's part in that little by-play.

'Sounds like Zip,' Yerby murmured when the other had finished. 'As mean and ornery as a sidewinder.'

'Why do you stay on with Arrow?' Lee asked curiously. He had already formed his judgment of this Bill Yerby and admired what he saw. Bill was not only a likeable man, but had every appearance of being a top-hand.

Yerby grinned sheepishly and shrugged his massive shoulders. 'Dunno, Kells. Habit maybe. I bin with Frank a long time. Seen him take on all these gun-handy gents like Putnam and Kessel and Beston.'

'Were you with Frank when he first came to Creation River, Bill?' Kells asked.

Yerby puffed at his cigarette. 'What we doin' yappin' on the door-step? Come inside an' I'll rustle cawffee and somethin' to eat.'

Kells followed the other inside the neat-looking shack with its two rows of double bunks, cook-stove, table and boxes.

Yerby paused in the act of feeding fresh wood to the stove. 'I joined up with Arrow soon after Frank came to the Bend,' he said. 'George was already with him. Heerd tell they trailed up from San Saba Valley or some such place.'

'The San Saba Valley?' Kells echoed softly, half to himself. 'That's the last piece I've been missing in the jig-saw puzzle.'

Chapter Nine

NOCTURNAL VISITORS

Dusk had given way to darkness by the time Lee and Bill had finished their meal and cleared away.

Over supper, Lee had sounded Bill out and was satisfied that Yerby, as he put it himself, 'owed no loyalty to a cut-throat outfit of bushwhackers.'

'What you figure on doing then, Bill?' Kells asked later as the two men squatted on a felled tree a few yards from the cabin.

Yerby shrugged and grunted and then spat into the darkness.

'If what you tell me is all true, Lee, and I ain't doubtin' it, I'd figure I was due to get my time an' quit Arrow once and for all. Point is more, what you figure on doin', ain't it? You cain't very well go back an' brace Frank while he's got a bunch o' gunsels at his back.

'And here's another thing. You got Frank figured out now, well, supposin' he's got you figured out too? You thought o' that? You ain't changed yore name remember. It's more'n likely he's been doin' a mite o' thinkin' an' possible he's recollected that name o' yours from way back.'

Kells nodded and commenced to roll a cigarette. He had thought of that too, and whilst he was determined to make Frank Shane pay the full price for Ezra Kells' death, he was not particularly anxious to throw his own life away – certainly not before he had settled with Frank.

'The trail-herd'll be due to start for Hide City in a few days, Bill,' Kells said slowly. 'Reckon with most of the hands gone it will level out the odds a bit.'

Yerby nodded. 'An' with me to side you–'

'This isn't your fight, Bill, 'though I appreciate–'

Lee's words stopped suddenly as the faint drumming of hoofs came to the ears of both men.

Yerby got to his feet, his gaze going to the

135

lamplit cabin where his rifle lay. But instead of moving towards the building, he drew the six-gun from its holster and thumbed back the hammer.

Kells was on his feet now, crossing over to a tangle of brush the other side of the clearing in front of the cabin.

Now, anyone approaching would be caught between two fires...

'Sure burnin' leather, whoever it is,' Yerby whispered across to the brush.

Kells didn't reply. Judging by the thundering rataplan of hoofs as the horse raced nearer, Bill Yerby's remark was almost an understatement.

Whoever it was riding this way, was doing so at a killing pace.

With a final crescendo of noise the rider burst into view, a vague shadowy figure atop a faltering horse only just identifiable in the clear starlight.

Now the rider was a bare twenty yards from the lamplit cabin, as he slid from leather and automatically trailed the reins over the trembling beast's head.

'Lee! Lee!'

For a moment, Kells stood transfixed. Then he moved out from the shadows, holstering his gun. He strode forward, glimpsing now the slim, half-swaying figure of Anna Collier.

He saw her face, white as the shirt blouse she wore; the fair hair tumbling about her shoulders, loosed from the restraint of pins during that wild night ride across the range.

'Lee!' She half sobbed his name, moving forward and gripping his arms as though to make certain he was flesh and bone. Yerby, too, moved out from the shadows and Anna recognized him with a sudden start.

'What's happened, Anna?' Kells said, and when the girl hesitated, added. 'Bill's okay, you can talk in front of him.'

'It's Zip,' Anna got out at last. 'Not only Zip but Frank as well. But Zip's coming–'

'Let's go inside and calm down,' Lee said taking the girl's arm and putting his own around her trembling body.

'I'll see to the horse if he ain't dead already,' Yerby said with sardonic humour. 'Be in presently.'

Lee nodded and led the girl into the cabin. He sat her on one of the upturned boxes which did service as chairs and without a word produced a pint bottle of whisky from his saddle-roll.

He uncorked the bottle and held the neck to her pale lips. 'Drink some, Anna.'

She sipped some of the burning spirit, gagged and managed to swallow a sizeable shot. A little colour swam into her face.

Lee turned up the lamp slightly and sat on a box near the table.

'Now, Anna, what's the trouble?' he demanded. 'What's this about Frank and

Zip Cantrell?'

She said, her low voice now more controlled. 'I overheard Zip and Frank planning this thing, Lee. Zip's coming out here to settle with you – kill you, and Frank's given his approval.

'I heard Frank tell Cantrell that he had you figured as the son of a man he had had a set-to with years ago, back in the – where was it? – the San Saba Valley, I think.'

Kells nodded grimly and turned his head as Bill appeared in the doorway.

'Take a pew, Bill. Anna's jus told me Zip's gunning for me and Frank's found out who I am. The set-to he had, Anna,' Lee said turning back to the girl, 'was a small matter of murder. Frank Shards–'

'Shards! I've heard that name before, I think. Wait! Yes, of course; that was Frank's name years ago before he changed it to Shane. I'd never have remembered, I guess, if you hadn't mentioned it.'

'So you know Frank's the man you want,' Yerby said seating himself on the edge of his bunk, 'and now Frank's got on to you. Where do we go from there?'

Anna's glance shuttled from Bill to Lee. 'It looks like Bill is on our side,' she said. 'Is that right?'

Kells nodded and the girl went on. 'Zip's aiming to ride here to-night, but I didn't know what time. That's why I nearly killed my pony. He might be here any moment, Lee; we've got to be ready for him.'

Yerby said. 'We'll be ready, Anna, but if I know Zip for the sneakin' coyote he is, he'll arrive later, much later, and try and get Lee with his pants down.'

'I'd figure it that way too,' Kells agreed, 'but we'll start getting our reception committee ready right soon. Zip will have to play it carefully because he knows you'll be here, Bill, and he won't know quite how you'll set in on this. That means he'll be doubly cautious; probably wait 'till he figures we're asleep.'

'Then I guess I needn't have lathered my horse,' Anna said with a shaky laugh.

Lee looked at her. She was damned beautiful limned like that in the lamplight with the gleaming hair like a halo of gold, her face white and taut and her eyes dark and smoky-blue with her thoughts.

Kells stood up and leaned forward grasping her soft arms gently.

'Don't think I'm ungrateful for what you've done, Anna, just because I'm taking this calmly. I had a hunch that maybe Frank was on to me, same as I'm on to him, now. What I didn't know, of course, was Zip coming here to kill me like the paid gunsel he is.'

Anna nodded. 'My trouble was I couldn't get away until later in the day. Every time I went to saddle my horse, Zip or Cal or someone seemed to be watching me. Not that they would have stopped me, probably, but I wanted to ride out unseen.'

Kells produced the whisky again and this time poured a little into a tin mug. He shoved the mug over to the girl and poured a slug each for himself and Yerby.

Presently Lee said, 'You'd best get back, Anna. No sense in you waiting around here. Bill and I will handle this business. How you going to explain your absence to Frank?'

She smiled. 'Don't worry about that. I'll find some tale for him to swallow. I may not even run into him.'

She stood up and Lee said. 'You'll have to ride your own horse back, Anna, if you possibly can. We switch mounts and the Arrow men'll spot it and figure out you've been here.'

Bill turned to the girl. 'I rubbed your horse down, Anna, an' fed and watered it. It's had a good coupla hours rest. You should make it back all right if you're plumb keerful.'

Anna nodded as Bill left the cabin to throw her rig on the pony. For a moment Lee and Anna were alone, in a lamplit cabin, far out on the night-shadowed range.

She put her arms about his neck and kissed him and Lee felt himself caught up for the moment in a wild surge of passion.

Strangely, the thought of Lea Franchot came to his mind and her face swam before his eyes, blotting out the golden vision of

Anna Collier.

She sensed his sudden preoccupation and drew away. 'I'm sorry, Lee.'

'I guess I'm the one to be sorry,' he murmured as she turned towards the door.

The moon had long since come up and had half completed its journey to the south-west, when the faint sounds of an approaching rider whispered across the still night to the north-western cabin wherein gleamed a single coal-oil lamp.

Zip Cantrell slid quietly from leather some fifty-sixty yards from the cabin and tied reins to a sapling.

He drew the black six-gun from its holster, thumbing back the hammer and spinning the cylinder. Satisfied with the action, he eased the hammer down and walked with jerky yet silent tread towards the darkly silhouetted cabin. He was not surprised that a soft light glowed through the open door. He could see that the lamp was dim and evidently Kells and Yerby had turned in, leaving the lamp merely turned low, in preference to extinguishing it completely.

There was nothing unusual in this – a practice invariably followed in the bunkhouse. It saved fumbling for matches in the dark if a man wanted a smoke during the night or in case of any sudden emergency which necessitated the crew being suddenly roused.

The black figure of Zip Cantrell moved forward softly, the moonlight glinting on the naked gun in his right hand. Within the space of a few moments, he was across the threshold and inside the cabin.

The lamp cast sufficient light for the sinister gunman to glimpse the two blanket-covered figures on the right-hand bunk. The shape on the top cot stirred, and Bill Yerby's face blinked owlishly in the half light.

'What the hell goes on?' he demanded sleepily. 'Who is it? Say, Zip! What in heck air you doin' with that gun?' Bill Yerby surprise seemed every bit the perfect product, though he eyed Zip Cantrell narrowly and grasped his own gun more firmly under cover of the blankets.

Zip put a finger to his lips enjoining the other to silence. 'I'm lookin' for a rat called Kells,' Cantrell whispered, 'and I reckon I've found him!' He pointed with his gun to the lower bunk and Yerby nodded as though confirming Zip's surmise.

Then Cantrell took a step back, curled forefinger through the trigger-guard and fired rapidly into the huddled figure on the lower bunk.

It was certainly a realistic shape, even to the dun-coloured stetson over the head, but Zip Cantrell felt a trickle of cold fear as the bullets smashed clean through the blankets into the woodwork of the bunk. It was like

142

shooting at a ghost. And then the stetson, jolted by the ripping slugs slid down revealing the horn of a saddle.

With a startled loath, Cantrell began to turn.

'Hold it, Zip!' The voice came from behind and froze the very marrow of Zip Cantrell's bones.

He stood like a statue, half-turned, his gun still out-thrust and smoking. Powder fumes hung white on the still air inside the cabin, filling the room with their unmistakably acrid bite.

'Drop your gun, Zip!' Again the words, though softly spoken were overlaid with such deadly menace that even the hardened little killer shivered.

He racked his mind, trying to remember how many bullets he had fired. Had he fired all six? He could not remember.

He heard the tell-tale metallic click as the man behind him thumbed back the hammer and Zip Cantrell dropped the Colt with a crash. His hands came up, but not quite in the same way as one would expect.

Bill Yerby was moving off the bunk now, six-gun revealed as he swung hands and legs into view.

Cantrell half-stooped, and whirled with amazing speed, reaching for the hide-out gun under his shoulder. He was round now, facing the grim figure of Lee Kells. In Zip's lean right hand was a Colt .38 which, even in the act of swinging it round and up, he fired with a desperately urgent speed.

Kells fired too, a fraction of a second before, and both bullets from Lee's gun found their target in Zip's chest. But Cantrell's one and only bullet had pierced Lee's left thigh and Kells staggered back from the force of that .38 slug at such close range.

Zip's body was spun half around from the impact of the two .45 bullets. He was dead even before he hit the floor.

Bill lowered his gun slowly and finally sheathed it.

'That was fast triggerin', Lee, and just as well, else that rat might have done even more damage with that hide-out gun.

'Let's look at that leg of yours. Zip'll keep for a while.'

Kells grunted and sat down on an upturned box at the table. He laid his gun in front of him and painfully unbuckled and stripped off his chaps.

His face was pale in the lamplight and Bill turned up the wick, pulling the lamp towards him before commencing an inspection of Lee's wound.

There was a deal of blood, but the bullet had gone clean through the outer, fleshy part of the thigh.

Bill made his careful examination of the wound and before cleansing and binding it, gave Lee a stiff shot of whisky.

Yerby used some of the spirit on the wound, made a wad with a clean handkerchief of Lee's and bound it tightly in position.

This was by no means the first gun-shot case that Bill Yerby had attended to.

He finished the bandaging with a grunt of satisfaction.'

'Reckon that'll be all right, Lee, though it'll hurt a bit for a time and be stiff by mornin'.'

Kells grinned, feeling better now that the blood had been stopped in its steady flowing.

'Morning can't be so far away at that, Bill.'

Yerby nodded and gave a sly grin. 'Sounds like a hint for me to rustle up breakfuss an' cawfee. I'll get the stove goin' fust an' while that's pullin, get Cantrell's body outside.'

Lee nodded. 'Point is, Bill, are we goin' to bury him here or lug him back to Arrow?'

Yerby fed wood to the stove, stuffed a screw of kerosene-soaked paper in and set a match to the fuel. In a few seconds the wood was blazing away. He placed a coffee-pot atop the stove then rolled and lit two cigarettes, handing one to Kells.

'It's a dead cert you cain't show your face at Arrow any more, Lee. We know from what Anna said that Frank's cottoned on to your game and who you are.

'You go back there, boy, and you'll be met with a hail of lead from the rest of Frank's gun-slicks.'

Lee nodded. 'You're right. But, like I said, they'll still make that trail-drive, I reckon.'

Yerby nodded. 'This whole thing's goin' to take some figurin' out, Lee. Reckon you want to even things up with Frank for the sake of your old man, but you cain't do it against a bunch of killers – and with that gun-shot wound too.'

Lee passed a hand wearily across his face. 'Reckon I'll hit the hay for a couple of hours, Bill. I feel kind of sleepy.'

Yerby said. 'You do that. I'll keep a weather-eye open. It's about four a.m. now. I'll wake you around seven, huh?'

Lee nodded and limped over to the lower bunk, drawing the bullet riddled blankets over him. He was asleep in a few seconds, no longer aware of the dull, steady throbbing in his leg...

Kells' leg was as stiff as a board and the pain was something to keep a man's teeth grinding together. Sweat beaded his face yet he finally managed to mount Red unaided.

Bill had lashed Zip's body to the *segundo's* own horse, now fresh after a night's rest and a good graze.

It was around eight when they left the cabin, having previously talked over their next move.

Bill was taking the *segundo's* body into

146

Arrow with a clear enough story, except that no reference would be made to Anna Collier's timely warning.

'Supposing they jump you, Bill?' Kells had remonstrated. 'Seems like you're rather shoving your head into a noose.'

Yerby was confident. 'They ain't got nuthin' on me, Lee. I'm aimin' to get my time and let 'em have Zip's body. That's all. Reckon I'll meet you in Lordville like we's arranged.'

Kells shook his head. 'I still don't like it. Frank'll be hoppng mad if he figures you had any part in helping me, Bill. I've killed two Arrow riders and wounded Schillinger. That's a mighty bad reputation to have earned.'

'Fust I knew was you'd shot Zip and was holdin' a gun on me,' Bill grinned. 'I was asleep, see? There was only one-two shots fired. Time I was awake, Zip was on the floor daid, and you'd lifted my gun.

'We rode down into the Bend jest like we are; you holdin' a gun on me all the time. That's the end of the story an' I'm stickin' to it. Frank cain't do anythin' about it, nor will any of his gunslingers. I ain't so slow on the draw myself.'

So it had finally been arranged and both men, with the third horse and its grim burden, made their way slowly across the range, nooning at a water-hole and hitting the Bend country by mid-afternoon. A mile or two

147

ahead they could see the shapes of the Arrow buildings.

Lee grasped Yerby's calloused hand.

'Good luck, Bill. See you later to-night in town. Better keep your hand near your gun when you talk to Frank.'

Yerby picked up the reins and the lead-line of Zip's pony. 'Don't you worry, boy. I'll be drinkin' with you before ten to-night.'

Lee watched as the Arrow man gently spurred his horse down the gradual slope which quartered to the ranch buildings. Then Lee turned his own horse along the narrow trail to town. It wouldn't be a bad idea he thought to get Doc Ivory to look at his leg. He wanted it in good shape as soon as possible, for Lee knew that in a little while he would have a sizeable fight on his hands and one which could only culminate in either his own death, or Frank's.

Chapter Ten

ZIP CANTRELL COMES HOME

Though Anna's horse had been rested for less than three hours, the treatment it had received at Bill Yerby's hands had worked wonders.

He had removed every mark of sweat and foam, giving the animal a thorough rubbing down before feeding and watering it. But at that, Anna knew she would have to nurse her mount carefully during the long ride back to the ranch. At the same time she'd have to make what speed she could, because the later she arrived back, the more likely it was that questions'd be asked and suspicions aroused.

She knew this range pretty well, and taking advantage of that knowledge sought out every cut-off, every piece of easy, level ground that she could. The moon was up now, and Anna Collier had little difficulty in orienting herself and keeping to a crow-flight course. As she rode, she maintained a sharp lookout for Cantrell, just in case their paths should happen to cross.

But it was approaching three o'clock before she sighted the ranch buildings and noted the lights that still shone both from the house itself and the bunkhouse. Her mount was just about all in. Lame in one foot, sweat-streaked and trembling.

In the ranch yard, she turned the beast into the corral after stripping off the rig and throwing a blanket over its back.

She closed the gates quietly and moved towards the house. A figure loomed up, big and foreboding, from the gallery and Frank Shane watched her cross the moonlit yard to the house.

For the first time there was no courtesy in his attitude to Anna Collier. She knew by his opening words and their very tone, that Frank had changed. There was anger in his face and even in the moonlight she could see temper stain his cheeks and sparkle in his cold eyes.

'Where in hell have you been?' he demanded and Anna felt a thin sliver of fear, such as she had not experienced with Frank Shane before.

'I got lost, Frank.' She spoke with a forced calm and laughed convincingly as though deriding herself for such foolishness.

'You got lost?' Frank's voice was harsh with anger; cold with suspicion and disbelief. 'Don't lie, Anna. You know this range nigh on as well as the men, leastways most of them. I want to know where you been.'

He took her arm, propelling her inside the house to the big living room in which a wood fire crackled in the hearth. He crossed over to the lamps, turned them up, flooding the room with light.

Anna saw the half-empty whisky bottle and the ash-tray of half-smoked cigars. Frank was worrying and she knew it was because he was wondering whether Zip had succeeded in killing Lee Kells.

She determined to wrest the initiative from Frank by attacking him.

'You've no right to talk to me like that,

Frank. Accusing me of lying. I'm not one of your paid gun-slingers.'

'Never mind about that.' Shards' voice was still rough, his face ugly with suspicion. 'You tell me what you been doin' out on the range 'till this time in the mornin'.'

There was every mark of utter weariness in her face and figure, yet she faced him boldly, her head lifted, her cold hands tightly clenched.

'I felt like riding to-night, Frank. You may not have noticed but I haven't been out much lately; there's not much to occupy a girl at Arrow. I crossed the river and wandered north-eastwards—'

'North-east?'

She nodded, knowing why Frank was so concerned about that direction.

'It's pretty broken country farther over,' she explained. 'I guess you know that. Arroyos, rock gullies and brush-tangled draws. Like I said, I got lost, and wandered about for hours. Then my pony went lame. When I did finally find the trail, it was as much as I could do to get it to move at all. Sometimes I had to walk alongside.

'Now, if you've finished questioning me, I guess I'd like to turn in. I'm dead tired.'

Shane bit at a fresh cigar, lighting it with a sulphur match.

'Zip rode out last night. He hasn't returned yet. I wondered whether you might have met up with him along the trail.'

She had been waiting for this question and now, facing him squarely, she lied like a trooper.

'I didn't meet up with anyone. I only wish I had. It sure would have saved me a heap of trouble. Why what do you think's happened to Zip? Where's he gone so late at night?'

Frank's suspicions had at least been lulled by the girl's apparently sincere and truthful explanations. He was not entirely satisfied; on the other hand, he could find no way of poking holes in Anna's story. In the absence of any witnesses, it was her word against his suspicions, but his mind was already returning to Zip Cantrell and Lee Kells.

'All right,' he grunted at last. 'You'd best get to bed.'

Anna departed thankfully. She did not realise until she was ascending the stairs, how much her heart was pounding and how badly her limbs were trembling. She had never seen Frank in quite such a mood as this, for all his rough ways. She was scared, and she knew too, that Frank Shane alias Frank Shards, was scared too. Scared of a nester's son named Lee Kells.

But the Arrow owner was in for a greater shock still, later that day.

Shane had spent a few fitful hours in bed, worrying about the way things were shaping. He had hardly expected Zip back much before dawn; probably the *segundo* would snatch a few hours sleep with saddle and blanket, out on the range. And yet...

Frank stirred restlessly, his body tired, his brain over-active with anxiety. It had been a fool thing to do, he now considered, to engage Kells as foreman, after the man had wounded George and shot down Foley Kessel. And that woman, Marion Starr, dam' her! She it had been who had settled Luke Putnam's hash and then Race Arnold turning around blandly and saying it was a kind of self-defence and no law could touch a woman under those circumstances.

Frank began to find excuses for his own actions. It had seemed a good thing to make Kells foreman. George had been getting a mite too uppish for a long time – so had Luke and Foley – and this Lee Kells seemed to be a tough waddy who could handle a tough crew.

How could he have known that Kells was the son of that two-bit nester in the San Saba Valley who they had lynched because he threatened to blab their plans to Crockett?

It was well after dawn when Frank Shane at last fell into a troubled sleep and when he awoke the sun was past the meridian.

He washed and shaved hurriedly, anxious to see Zip and ascertain from the *segundo* what had happened. He wanted to see the dead body of Kells and satisfy himself that there was no further need to fear this tough, grim-visaged rider.

Frank descended the stairs and made his way to the kitchen, pouring himself a cup of coffee from the pot on the stove. The thought of any food was nauseous at the moment, so he lit a cigar, and tried to curb his impatience whilst he drank the scalding liquid.

He noticed that the hands of the kitchen clock pointed to a quarter of four, as he emerged from the rear door of the house and crossed the wide yard towards the outbuildings. He saw Cal Beston and Eddie Hindel leading their horses towards the blacksmith shop where Charlie Heyman stood, a smoke-blackened leather apron about his middle.

'Howdy, boys,' Frank called as the two hands waited for Shane to approach. 'Zip come in yet?'

Eddie turned questioning eyes to Cal Beston. 'You seen him, Cal?' Beston shook his head. 'Not since early last night. Said he had a chore to do and rode out. We kinda figured he was taking a look-see to Clayton's Strip – make sure it was really stripped.'

The men laughed and Frank fought down the sudden panic and fear which threatened to rise in his gorge. He managed a weak smile. 'You tell him I want to see him, when he comes in Charlie,' he said to the blacksmith.

Heyman nodded. 'Rest of the boys are out with the trail-herd, boss,' he said. 'Flip's in charge.'

Frank grunted and Cal Beston said, 'Maybe this is Zip. Rider comin' in leadin' a spare horse. Looks like – by cripes, it is–'

All glances turned swiftly towards the rider now descending a distant ridge.

For a long moment there was tight, hard-packed silence.

It was Eddie Hindel who spoke in his thin, expressionless voice.

'That ain't Zip,' he said slowly. 'It's Bill Yerby from the line-cabin an' he's packin' a dead or wounded hombre across t'other horse, or I'm a Chinese bastard.'

Frank Shane felt his mouth and throat go dry. The taste of the cigar sickened him and he threw it to the ground. All eyes remained steadily fixed on the oncoming rider. Minutes ticked by. Nobody moved. Cal's and Eddie's horses threw up their heads and nickered shrilly. The musical jingling of bridle bits was a raw, discordant sound to Frank's ears.

'It's Bill, fer sure,' Charlie Heyman said presently, 'an' he's leadin' Zip's horse.'

It was nearly a half-hour later that Bill Yerby rode into the yard and, seeing the group at the blacksmith shop, put his horse in that direction.

He said, 'Howdy,' and four pairs of eyes

gazed back at him, bright with speculation.

Charlie Heyman's glance moved over the figure of Zip Cantrell lashed to the horse. 'So Zip ketched it at last,' he said and spat.

'Let's have it, Bill,' Frank said in a dangerously soft voice.

Yerby pushed back his hat and started to roll a cigarette.

'Reckon you know by now, Boss, that that Kells feller is sure chain-lightnin' with a gun.' It was like rubbing salt into Frank's wound and Shane snarled, 'Sure, get on with the story, Bill.'

Yerby found a match, drew it along the seat of his pants and applied the flame to his quirly.

'Fust thing I knew, Frank, was hearin' one-two shots in the middle of the night an' wakin' up to find Zip here, on the floor, and Kells standin' over him with a smoke-pole. My own gun was gone. Kells had lifted it. I couldn't do nuthin'. In any case it was too late. Time I got off'n the bunk, Zip was sure dead.'

'Was Zip the only visitor you had last night, Bill?' Frank demanded.

Yerby showed his surprise at the question. 'Why, yes, who else? Lessn' you're referring to Kells himself! He arrived 'bout sun-down or thereabouts. Told me what had happened to George an' that he had been ramroddin' the spread for a week–'

'Then what?' Frank said, licking his dry lips.

Yerby dismounted, trailing the reins of both horses. He leaned against his own mount's rig.

'We had cawffee and I cooked up a meal. Kells said for me to stay overnight and light out for the ranch in the mornin'.

'That was jake by me,' Yerby continued. 'Wasn't no point in ridin' through the night anyway. We washed up an' smoked an' talked 'till it was time to turn in.'

'What time was that, Bill?' Shane asked.

Yerby considered and scratched his bald spot. 'Didn't rightly notice, not havin' a time piece on me, but I'd say it was mebbe around eleven.'

'Yes?'

Yerby nodded. 'Before twelve anyway. Well, Kells gets into the bottom bunk and I take my usual top one. The other two behind the door are empty, see? We leave the lamp turned low on the table, well away from the door draught an' turn in.

'Like I said, fust I knew was gun-shots an' powder-smoke. Reckon I must have been sleepin' plumb peaceful. Took me a few seconds to kinda figure things out an' see what was what.

'There was Zip on the floor with a bullet hole in his chest an' Kells wavin' the gun at me an' tellin' me to take it easy. "Tried to

157

jump me, he did," Kells says, "but me bein'
a light sleeper, I heard his horse a way off.
Climbed outa bed an' waited fer him.""

Yerby paused and drew on his cigarette,
his bright glance flicking from face to face.
In the tight silence, a horse pawed the
ground and a bridle jingled. These were the
only noises.

'Kells had made up his blankets to look like
he was inside 'em,' Bill continued. 'Saw afterwards, several bullet holes, so it looked like
Zip jest natcherally cut loose with his hawg-
leg an' Kells came up behind him, called him
an' shot it out.' Yerby shrugged. 'Wasn't my
quarrel anyway and I'm tellin' you, Frank, I
ain't sorry Cantrell's dead. He was another
one of the Kessel-Putnam breed.'

Cal Beston's hand moved slowly to rest on
the butt of his gun and Yerby's hard glance
caught and held the other man's gaze. 'You
ain't figurin' on callin' me, are you Cal? You
ain't kinda hintin' I'm lyin' or anything'?'
There was a deadly under-current in Bill
Yerby's voice and Beston, remembering
things about Bill, recollecting the speed of
his draw, shook his head slowly and
withdrew his hand from his gun. 'No, Bill.
Way I see it, things musta happened 'bout
like you said. I reckon we all know that Kells
bustard is chain-lightnin' with a gun.
Another Johnny Ringo if you ask me.'

Eddie Hindel nodded his agreement, his

small, close-set eyes darting from one to the other. 'Reckon that's about the way it was, boys, like Bill told us. Then, come mornin' Kells ups and lights out, ain't that right, Bill?'

Yerby nodded. 'He made no secret of the fact he was headin' for Lordville. Fact was we rode together a piece; Kells gave me back my gun but without any shells. Looks like you'd best fix Zip up, boys, behind the barns.'

Frank let out his breath slowly; his face was grey in the bright sunlight. Yerby, more discerning than the rest, read fear in back of those cold, hard eyes.

'All right, Bill,' Shane said at last. 'You'd best eat an' then hit the hay for a couple hours.'

Bill shook his head. 'I'm quittin' Frank. You just give me my time.'

'Quittin'?'

'Sure! I've got the itch to ride on an' see a few places. Saved me some money, too over the past six-seven years.'

This was another shock for Frank. His crew was being steadily whittled down one way and another and he would need every cow-nurse and every gun-slinger he could lay hands on in the days to come. He had always been able to rely on Bill Yerby before. What had got into Bill now? Had it any connection with Lee Kells he wondered.

'So you want your time, Bill?' Frank said,

half sneering. 'Well there ain't no law that says you cain't be paid for what you've done, this bein' the last day of the month.'

Yerby agreed. 'I'll get my things from the bunkhouse.'

'You do that, an' come on over to the office,' Frank flung over his shoulder as he turned and walked with hurried steps across the yard. He had already forgotten Zip Cantrell's body slung across the horse, in his rage and bitterness at this latest development.

Lee Kells took his time riding towards town, his mind busy mainly with his own particular problem; the problem of dealing with Frank Shards alias Frank Shane.

But Lee found room in his thoughts for Anna Collier as well. He wondered whether she had been able to bluff Frank about where she had been last night. If Shane ever got on to the truth, then Anna's life would not be worth a row of beans, Kells thought sombrely. The same thing went for Bill Yerby, though the latter was obviously far better equipped to take care of himself than was Anna.

Bill could hold his own, Lee felt sure, but Anna Collier might be in a very dangerous position.

Twice during that early evening ride across Arrow land, Kells halted, undecided whether or not to make for the Arrow ranch house and fight it out with Frank, irrespective of how many gun-hands he had hanging around.

Only the prospect of being shot down and killed before his self-imposed chore of retribution could be discharged, persuaded Kells to continue on to Lordville...

It was not yet dusk when Lee hit town, tired in mind and body, his leg-wound aching abominably.

He made first for Doc Ivory's cottage, remembering vaguely its location from when Schillinger had been taken there to have his arm fixed.

Doc Ivory was a lean, stoop-shouldered man with a sour face, bisected by a nicotine-stained moustache.

He untied the bandage and probed about, not too carefully, until the sweat stood out on Lee's face.

'Seems clean enough,' Ivory grunted at last, 'but I'll put a fresh dressing on it. You're dam' lucky young man. Another inch or so and the femur would have been shattered.'

Fifteen minutes later, Kells limped out of the cottage. The doc had said to rest the leg for a week. Lee smiled grimly as he dragged it along the side street to Main. A fat chance there'd be of getting much rest during the next few days, he thought...

Kells' next call was to the sheriff's office. Lee figured he might catch the lawman in before his evening visit to Roper's saloon.

Race Arnold sat in his swivel-chair at the battered, paper-strewn desk and his grey glance lifted as Kells limped in through the door.

'Sit down and rest that leg, Kells,' he said. 'What's the trouble now?'

Lee slumped down into a chair, sticking out his left leg straight in front of him. He tried to remember how much he had told the Sheriff when he had first met him in Roper's salon and recollected that he had said precious little. He wondered whether to tell him the whole story now.

The hell with it! Kells thought, and began to give the lawman a brief word picture of everything that had transpired since he had lit out for the north-west line-cabin, leaving out only the episode concerning Anna Collier. The fewer people who knew about her visit to the cabin the better.

Race Arnold sighed, leaned back in his chair and re-lit the dead cigar stub in his mouth.

'Your middle name's certainly "Trouble," ain't it, Kells?' he grumbled. 'Fust you go an' bust Schillinger's arm, an' kill Foley Kessel. Oh, I know! Self-defence, sure! Then you tangle with Zip Cantrell an' kill him. Now you've found Frank Shane's the man you been after nigh on ten years. That'll mean more trouble, more killin'. One of you's goin' to get creased kinda permanent an' I've gotta shrewd idea who it's goin' to be. Maybe I can see my meal-ticket floatin' away. Maybe that might not be such a bad thing either. Give me a chance to cut loose from Arrow and their killers.'

Lee said. 'Bill Yerby will witness that I killed Cantrell in self-defence. Bill's quitting Arrow and meeting me right here in town to-night, if you want to see him.

'As for Zip I had no choice, Sheriff. It was like I told you.'

Arnold nodded, 'Sure, sure, I know. I'm not holding you, Kells. Be a waste of time if I did. No jury in Lordville would convict a man for shootin' Zip Cantrell any more'n they would for creasin' Schillinger or puttin' paid to Kessel an' Putnam. Reckon they's the worst of the bunch, though there's still Cal Beston, Flip Denkern, Charlie Heyman, Slim Tuckfold, Eddie Hindel and Bandy Hillinger. They're all bad medicine. Sol Schultz, Ray Lusgow, Phil Dukes, they ain't so bad. As for Yerby, why, I guess he's an all-right hombre. How he ever came to—' Arnold broke off, his mind busy with the new angles that Kells' news had produced.

'If this was Hide City, the county town,' the sheriff said presently, 'I'd tell you to get a lawyer, collect all your evidence together and let me arrest Frank Shane, or Shards, as you say he was called.' Race Arnold sighed heavily, 'As it is, Kells – well you can see there's little enough law in Lordville, with Arrow roddin' it over the whole of Creation Valley.' Arnold leaned forward. 'Maybe you heard, or maybe you ain't, Kells, but I've got a sick wife. I been keepin' her alive for years with expensive medicines and treatments. Why, man, three years ago the doctors gave her six months to live. Dunno why I'm tellin' you all this–'

'I can guess, Race,' Kells said. 'Your sheriff's pay isn't enough, not by a jugful, for all that expense. Heard tell you've got three nice kids, too. Frank Shards figured the same and pays you, probably more than your county pay, to do things for him.'

Arnold nodded. 'That's about the size of it, Kells. I'm not makin' excuses.'

Kells brought down his hand in an impatient gesture. 'You leave Arrow to me, Race. I promise you there'll be no murder or wholesale killings as far as I'm concerned. What Shards'll do now he knows about me, I can't even guess at the moment. As for your position, you sit tight. I've got a hunch things'll work out better than you expect.'

Race Arnold sat staring at the papers on his desk, long after Lee Kells had gone. It was kind of crazy, he knew, but he felt himself believing in this tough waddy who had already bucked several of Arrow's killers with no small success.

164

Presently, Arnold threw away his dead cigar. He was wondering what Kells'd meant when he'd talked about things working out– The sheriff sighed heavily and reached for his hat, glancing at the wall-clock. It was time he had a drink, he needed one…

Chapter Eleven

THE RAWHIDERS

Lee Kells had one quick drink in Roper's and crossed immediately to Starr's Restaurant.

Lights were beginning to spring up in stores, shops, saloons and restaurants.

He grinned at Marion Starr as he threaded a way between the tables.

'Hallo, Lee,' she smiled as he reached the counter. 'Don't look at me, I guess I must look awful. I've been helping Gil with the evening cooking. But never mind that. You were limping, Lee. What's happened?'

Kells glanced around the restaurant. It was early as yet and most tables were empty. One or two men nodded at Lee or flipped their hands in greeting.

Two lean-faced youngsters sat at a table apart. They were like enough almost to be twins, certainly brothers. Kells' glance passed over them and then came back. They returned look for look with good measure.

'Who are the two youngsters with chips on their shoulders, Marion?'

'That's Bill and Jesse Rust. They run a few head on Clayton's Strip. You know? Near to Arrow land. Or at least they did. Came in to-night and said they were quitting.

'But tell me about yourself, Lee. We're not busy right now; come into the back for coffee and a meal.'

Lee thanked the girl, following her into the back kitchen in which he had sat after his first fight with the Arrow ramrod.

Gil Rabjohn, the cook, was busy at the stoves, with Lettie helping. She flashed him a shy glance and without waiting for instructions, poured Lee a cup of coffee and set it on the table before him.

'Thanks, Lettie,' Kells smiled. 'Maybe you'll have some tender steak and fried potatoes presently, huh?' She nodded brightly and Marion smiled as she sat at the table opposite Kells.

Lee rolled a cigarette, sipped some of the coffee and started in telling Marion what had happened during the last week.

Her green-grey eyes widened with surprise as he told her about Zip and Bill Yerby and Frank himself.

'So Frank really is the man you're after, Lee?'

He nodded and smiled thinly. 'I guess he's after me, too, seeing that I've killed Zip and Kessel and winged George, and he also knows who I am. Say, Marion, you've had no trouble with Arrow since you helped me – saved my life, I reckon– by killing Luke Putnam?'

She shook her head. Once again, Lee watched the red-gold lights dancing in her chestnut hair.

'Frank knew he couldn't do a thing about that, Lee. The whole town was behind us. As for George, why, I guess so long as he's laid up– Have you seen the doc about that leg-wound, Lee?'

Kells nodded. 'That's all fixed. Listen, Marion, I'm interested in those two boys from Clayton's strip. I'd like to talk to them. I'll come back here later for my food.'

She nodded and Kells left the kitchen, crossing the restaurant to where the two Rust brothers ate their meal in gloomy silence.

Kells drew up a chair and sat down opposite them.

'Which of you's Bill and which one Jesse?' he asked.

'Who wants to know?' It was the darker of the two men who asked the question.

'Lee Kells.'

'Lee Kells, eh?' The reaction was immediate. Bill and Jesse Rust were interested and the name meant something as was obvious not only by their expressions but by their following remarks.

The darker one put down his knife and fork and gazed at Kells steadily.

'I'm Jesse Rust. Thisyer's Bill, my brother. Guess you're the pilgrim we bin hearin' about. Shot up thet bustard, Schillinger, an' beat Foley Kessel in a rigged play.'

Kells nodded. A thin smile tugged at the corners of his wide mouth.

'Maybe you haven't heard Zip Cantrell came gunning for me.'

'Zip Cantrell? You mean he's daid?' Where there had been mild interest before, there was now a rapt, intense concentration on their faces.

'Guess we ain't heard that, Kells,' Bill said. 'But I'd shore admire to shake hands with the gent who's whittled down that crew of coyotes–'

'Me, too.' Jesse said extending a lean, brown hand across the table.

'What's the trouble?' Kells said drinking the coffee which Lettie had carried in from the kitchen. He rolled and lit a cigarette. In back of his mind was the beginnings of an idea. It concerned these two men – if they were willing. There was a way in which Frank might be brought out into the open and the rest of the Arrow killers smashed for good. But Lee's gaze had taken in the patched leather-work of these men; the gun-butt plates mended with rawhide instead of screws; spurs too, such as they were, were lashed on down-at-heel boots with rawhide thongs in the absence of buckles.

These men were rawhiders and the description, like that of nesters, was intended to be more derogatory than complimentary...

Jesse Rust pushed back his empty plate, fumbling for tobacco. Kells threw his Bull Durham across the table.

'We ran eighty-ninety head o' cattle on Clayton's Strip. Maybe you knew, Kells, maybe not. Arrow's been stealin' us blind, a few at a time. Shane wants to swallow Clayton's Strip along with other Arrow range. He figgers to spread out north-east across the river. Clayton's Strip's something of a stumbling block.

'He couldn't take the land from us. We got title deeds fer that from Uncle Sam; but he could and has stole us blind, so we ain't got no stock to run.'

'You had any fights with Arrow riders?'

Bill's laugh was scornful. 'Sure, whenever we could get our sights lined on 'em, but the rustlin' was always at night, the men masked, and 'less Jesse an' me was to sit up all night, week after week, we couldn't nohow watch all our stock and range. Clayton's Strip ain't so small, Mister Kells.

'And whenever we saw Arrow riders in daylight and accused 'em, they jest laughed and

169

told us to be right careful of our tongues…'

'In any case, Lee,' Jesse chipped in, 'while we're both ready to sling lead with the next man, two of us ain't no match fer fourteen-fifteen paid killers.'

Kells smiled. 'Number's coming down in our favour boys.' He ticked off names with the index finger of his right hand. 'Schillinger's out of it for some time. Kessel's dead and so is Putnam thanks to that red-headed girl back there in the kitchen.'

'We heard that.'

Kells nodded. 'Now Zip's dead and Bill Yerby's joining forces with me. I'm meeting him right here in Lordville to-night! That leaves Frank Shane's crew at about nine men.' Lee paused and raked the two young faces before him with his hard gaze. 'Four against nine's a sight better odds than two against fifteen.'

For a long moment no one spoke or moved at the able. Behind them, in the restaurant, the buzz of conversation was a steady, droning background to their thoughts, and through it Kells's last words had rowelled with the savage sharpness of a spur.

Jesse's glance slid to his brother's face. Then both looked at Kells. Jesse Rust said, 'You suggestin' we might fight back at Arrow – together?'

'Do you want to quit and lose your ranch and eighty-ninety head of beef without

170

hitting back?'

'Show us the way Kells an' we'll hit back all right.'

Lee nodded. Rawhiders they might be. Youngsters they were, but given half a chance they were ready to buck Frank Shane and all he stood for.

'What's your outfit's brand?' Lee asked presently.

Bill gave a crooked grin. 'Reckon folks have called us "Shoestring" so long, or the Clayton's Strip outfit, we almost plumb forget we got a registered brand. Oak-leaf it is, Kells, why?'

Lee sat for a moment in deep thought. Automatically his fingers shaped and lit another cigarette.

'Reckon I've seen some of your cattle over in the holding pens on Arrow land. There's another thing. They're figuring on trail-herding a bunch to Hide City in a couple days. Its unlikely there'll be more than two night guards at most.' Kells leaned forward. 'If we cut out the same number of cattle you've had stolen and change the Arrow brand like this–' Lee sketched rapidly on a piece of paper with a stub of pencil, drawing an arrow on its own

and then deftly adding a couple of

flourishes on either side.

He looked up and smiled. 'You've got your Oak-leaf critturs back, then, haven't you? It shouldn't be too difficult with a running iron and you'll only be taking back what has already been stolen from you.'

Jesse and Bill exchanged glances, their faces breaking into slow grins. Jesse took a deep breath. 'When do we start, Lee?'

Kells said, 'Get back to Clayton's Strip and re-occupy your ranch house. Draw me a map on back of this paper to show me how to get there. I'll come out later to-night with Bill Yerby. We'll give an owl hoot twice, then once.

'Get in some stores–' Kells stopped as a slow stain spread across Jesse's lean cheeks.

'Guess you're about broke, huh?' Lee reached into his pockets and placed a handful of ten-dollar gold pieces on the gingham table cloth. 'That should be enough for stores and shells as well. You got carbines?'

'I have,' Jesse said. 'Bill's is broke.'

'There's enough *dinero* there,' Lee said. 'Make out you're leaving the country if you like, then head back to your own place.

'Me and Yerby'll be with you later on. You on?'

'We're on,' the brothers gritted in unison.

Lee stood on the board-walk, hands thrust deep into the pockets of his coat. He wondered, as he had done more than once recently, whether he were playing this thing the smart way. Whatever else happened, he was determined to get Frank Shards, but at one and the same time he figured it was possible to help these rawhiders, perhaps even to recovering their cattle.

With an imperceptible shrug, Lee Kells crossed Main Street, threading a way through the nightly traffic to Roper's saloon, the rendezvous he had suggested to Yerby earlier on.

Bill was at the bar and his round face broke into a grin as he sighed Kells pushing through the batwing doors.

'Howdy, Lee,' he said pushing a bottle and shot glass towards the other. 'What's the news?'

Kells glanced about him. Mostly men were busy with their talk. One or two lifted a hand in greeting, recognising him, and Lee acknowledging their greetings, turned back to Yerby, knowing that their talk could not be heard over the babble of conversation.

He told Bill about the rawhiders and how Jesse and Bill were prepared to fight back if Lee would only show them how.

'Arrow's been stealing them blind,' Kells finished. 'Lifted about eighty-ninety head.'

'I know,' Yerby said. 'That's another thing I cain't stummick. Oh, sure, I ain't above clappin' my brand on a maverick or a spring calf if it's a big spread. Reckon a good many cattle barons started thetaway, but stealin' from a shoestring outfit like Oak-leaf, well it seems kinda like takin' somethin' from a cripple.

'Every man's got a right to live provided he can and does work,' Yerby continued. 'Ain't right that men like Frank – but enough o' that. What we goin' to do, Lee? I'm ready to side you. Figger I ain't got much to lose.'

'You might have something to gain by it,' Lee said cryptically. 'Here's what we do...'

It was about nine o'clock when Kells and Yerby rode out of Lordville, Lee taking the lead and following the trails Jesse Rust had drawn on his map.

They found the fording place at the Creation, without much difficulty, and though the moon was not yet up, the sky was like luminous buttermilk with the billions of winking stars.

Lee glanced at the Big Dipper, taking his bearings and heading north across the river through tangled chaparral brush at first. Later chaparral and thorn thickets gave way to sage-covered range. This north-eastern section was rougher country than the other parts of the valley that Kells had seen, but it was still good enough cattle country for a smallish outfit. Between the broken and undulating upthrusts were wide expanses of grassland, and water, in the shape of the twisting Creation River, was abundant.

'We should be getting close now, Bill,' Lee said reining his mount so that Yerby could come alongside.

Bill came up, peering through the darkness ahead towards and beyond a clump of trees silhouetted against the faintly paler surroundings.

'Looks like that might be a light ahead, Lee. Would they be showin' a light?'

'I didn't say for them not to,' Kells said. 'Arrow won't be looking for them I reckon, now Frank's taken their beef.'

Lee dropped the reins and cupped his hand to his mouth. The night air was shattered by the sudden piercing hoot of an owl. Twice in quick succession and then a third cry.

From beyond the clump of trees came a faint hooting in reply. Kells judged the ranch was about a quarter-mile away. He spurred the paint onwards then, towards the trees which presently became identifiable as a clump of live-oaks. Both men could now see the faint light filtering from the ramshackle building ahead. These boys were not hiding, Kells thought, but neither were they advertising their presence.

Hoofs clattered on the gravel of the yard

as Lee and his partner trotted their mounts out of the shadows of the live-oaks.

'Sing-out!' a voice commanded and almost immediately came the metallic click of a lever-action carbine.

'It's Kells and Yerby,' Lee called softly. 'Point that cannon the other way, Jesse.'

A low chuckle greeted this sally and shortly boots pounded on the squeaking boards of the porch steps as Jesse Rust descended and showed himself in the starlight. Away to the east the moon was rising, as yet, no more than a soft halation of gold in the star-speckled sky.

Jesse held the Winchester in the crook of his arm as Kells and Yerby slid from leather.

'There's a corral in back,' Jesse said, turning to show the way.

Kells nodded, following on behind with Bill bringing up the rear, both men leading their horses.

'Reckon we'll just water them and give a little feed,' Kells suggested. 'Leave them in the stable and not turn them loose in the corral.'

Jesse's brow rose. 'You ridin' again tonight, Lee? Bill's fixin' grub for you and we've got a coupla shakedown beds on the floor for you and Yerby.'

Kells grinned. 'Sorry I forgot to introduce you two. Bill, meet Jesse Rust.'

The two men solemnly shook hands. Then

Kells returned to Rust's question.

'I figure we'd best locate that trail-herd to-night, Jesse, if you and Bill are willing. For one thing, that herd was scheduled to move Saturday and I don't reckon Frank'll pass up the *dinero* on a thousand head just because Zip's lying underneath the ground.'

'Secondly,' Bill Yerby chipped in, 'the moon's comin' up and some cloud from the north-east by the look o' things. That should just make it right for us.'

Jesse grinned, showing white teeth.

'Then all we want's a good downpour to wash out the tracks an' everythin'll be jake.'

Lee said, loosening the cinch-strap on his rig. 'I don't say it'll be that easy, but I don't see why we shouldn't pull it off.'

Jesse nodded. 'C'm on inside and have some cawfee.'

The ranch house was pretty bare inside. Kells could see that these two game youngsters must have had a tough time during recent months.

It was a single-storied effort with a wood-shingle roof and walls of unpeeled fir logs. There was a fair-sized living room, a smaller work-room, a kitchen complete with stove and a pair of battered rockers and a biggish bedroom in the back.

Now, in the light of coal-oil lamps, the four men gathered around the kitchen to eat and discuss their plans for the raid.

Bill Rust had been busy opening canned goods from their newly purchased stores.

'You get your carbine, Bill?' Kells said.

'Sure,' Bill Rust grinned. He crossed to the corner of the room and picked up a shining new Winchester, handing it to Kells who inspected it critically, sighting it and testing the action.

'Looks all right, Bill. Hope you can use it!'

'I'm especially good at skunk-shooting, Lee. Don't usually reckon to miss...'

It was nearing midnight when the four men mounted and turned their ponies' heads towards Arrow range.

There was not overmuch talk. Plans, such as they were, had been discussed and understood and each man knew that always on such a chore as this, was the possibility that one or more of them might not return alive.

Jesse took the lead, with Lee and Bill Yerby close behind. Bill Rust watched their back-trail, the stock of the new carbine protruding from the worn scabbard under his right leg.

The clouds had blown up from the north-east as Yerby had anticipated and occasionally they'd dim the moon in its night journey to the west. So far, the weather conditions were perfect for the four Oak-leaf men.

Only the intermittent jingle of bridle chains and the occasional soft squeak of leather broke the silence, apart from the muted hoof-beats on the springy grass. Arrow grassland, Kells soon realised, and smiled grimly at the thought that technically they were trespassing.

Soon Lee brought his horse up alongside Jesse's mount.

'You know where we are, Jesse?'

Rust's gaze squinted ahead against the now darkening night.

'Reckon the buildings is about two-three miles ahead. Yeah! You can just see the Bend where the trees line it, sweepin' round to the north. Can you take over from here?'

Kells said. 'Sure! This is where we bear right. If the herd's still in the same place it's not far away. If it isn't,' he grinned into the darkness, 'we're on a wild-goose chase.'

There, in the dip, he vaguely remembered from his first few days at Arrow, a big herd was bedded down and suddenly, like a flash-back, he remembered the whole terrain and the cabins which was used by the night guards, particularly in bad weather.

But the night was still fine and the men might be out riding herd. Or, as the last thing they would expect were callers, they might quite well be playing cards in the cabin.

Lee waited for the others to reach him and gave them his suggestions.

Yerby shook his head. 'Don't cotton on to the idea of you tacklin' the cabin alone, Lee. Maybe one man, maybe two, maybe more.

179

Who can tell? Them odds ain't to my likin'. Sooner I came with you.'

The Rust brothers agreed with this, but recognising Lee as the leader, left the final decision to him.

'We'll ride nearer to the dip and hitch our horses, Bill,' Kells said to Yerby. 'I'll go on ahead to the cabin. If things go wrong, you'll be close behind to back me up, but I don't aim to deal in half measures.'

Yerby grudgingly agreed. Jesse and Bill Rust watched as Lee and Yerby moved off into the darker shadows of the range.

Near the dip they ground-tied their ponies and now Lee could see a light coming from the window of the cabin. The shack itself was about a half-mile from the bedded-down herd.

With a warning gesture to Bill, Lee angled across the scrub-dotted grassland towards the cabin. He moved quickly and silently, for all his high-heeled boots and long-rowelled spurs.

He glanced behind, making out the dim, blocky shape of Yerby following, a short distance back. Then he pulled the bandana up over his face masking it to the eyes. The wide brim of his hat was already tugged well down so that nothing of Kells' face was left visible.

The clouds were now blowing up more thickly, for the most part obscuring the moon, so that the cabin would have been almost invisible had it not been pin-pointed to Kells and Yerby by the thin sliver of chrome light spilling out from the gunny sack covered window.

The door, Lee discovered, was almost closed but fortunately not latched. He put a foot on the step and with his gun out and cocked, pushed quickly on the door.

He was inside before the men at the table had had time even to drop their cards. In the lamplight surprise stamped its almost comical shape on their faces. Immediately, Kells recognised Flip Derkern, and Sol Schultz. He moved forward quickly keeping away from the inner circle of lamplight, having no particular desire for these men to identify him.

'What the hell–,' Schultz growled, half rising and making a move with his right hand.

'Hold it!' Kells rasped. 'Stand up and turn around – the both of you.'

Under the menace of that unwavering black gun-barrel, Schultz and Denkern had no option but to comply with the harshly growled commands.

They had scarcely turned their backs, hands held at shoulder level, before Lee had whipped Denkern's gun from its holster and had brought the barrel of his gun crashing down on the Arrow man's head just behind the right ear.

For a split second, Sol Schultz had his chance and took it, diving for his gun and weaving out from underneath Kells' descending gun. Denkern hit the floor with a crash at the same time as Sol's gun spat flame and a bullet ricocheted off the edge of the table, missing Kells by an inch.

Before Schultz could trigger again, Lee had dived at him, gripping the man's gun wrist and clouting him savagely on the upraised arm with the barrel of his Colt.

Schultz grunted and cursed with pain. The gun-sight had cut through his shirt-sleeve like a knife through butter, gashing his forearm and leaving it momentarily useless.

There was a blinding flash of exploding light before Sol's screwed-up eyes as Kells' gun came crashing down on his unprotected head. Sol staggered and then dropped to the floor as Lee wheeled round towards the door. Yerby stood there, gun in hand and then both of them grinned suddenly.

'Help me to tie them up,' Lee said re-holstering his gun and replacing his bandana in its usual place at his neck.

It was a matter of minutes only before both unconscious men were securely trussed and gagged.

Kells turned the lamp low, took one last look at the inert figures and motioned to Yerby to precede him out of the cabin.

Chapter Twelve

NO SMOKE FROM THE SHACK

Kells saw the Rust brothers as two vague, almost indeterminate shadows some twenty paces away. He sensed their sharp fear and their hair-trigger anxiety which now prompted Jesse to call out in a voice that rose suddenly and shrilly in the silent night.

'Hold it an' reach!'

Kells smiled thinly; here was proof that for all their readiness to fight back, these boys had had little experience of action by night.

'Ease up, Jesse,' Kells said softly, moving forward with Yerby. 'The night guards are taken care of,' he continued. 'Wait'll we get our horses.'

Jesse let go his breath in a long sigh of relief, dipping the Winchester and replacing it in the saddle-scabbard. 'Thought Arrow had jumped you,' he explained with a note of apology in his voice.

Kells nodded, only afterwards realising that the movement would have gone by unseen in the darkness. He looked up at the scudding clouds, feeling the cooling breeze bringing with it a first few tentative drops of rain.

Yerby was returning with their mounts and Kells said, 'Let's go and cut out that eighty head.'

'Ninety,' Bill Rust murmured.

Kells let it go. Questioning folk didn't necessarily give you the truth. You either trusted a man or you didn't; same as he had trusted Bill Yerby.

The four moved off, riding as closely as possible, negotiating the down grade and coming up to the edge of the restless steers.

Most of these near ones were on their feet, made wary and uncertain by the approach of riders.

Kells said, 'You give them a hand at cutting out, Bill. I'll try and get the lead ones started.'

It was tricky work, rendered more delicate by the half-spooked mood of the beasts and the crowding darkness of the night. Only occasionally could Kells see the faint glow of the moon behind the scudding clouds and then he was busy dealing with the lumbering leaders as they were cut out and sent up the slope with an encouraging swipe from a coiled riata.

The rain became a thin drizzle which soon soaked men's shirts and trousers. None had brought a slicker with him. In spite of their having mentioned a downpour to erase tracks, no one had seriously contemplated even a brief break in the weather.

Once or twice Kells questioned himself

while his body reacted automatically to the task on hand. He could chase a dodging dogie and urge it back into line, even while his mind was caught up in speculation.

Speculation as to whether he were, after all, handling this thing the right way. He shrugged. For better or for worse he would go through with it now and if, in the process, such men as these rawhiders were helped to get on their feet, helped to fight instead of quit and to reclaim what was rightfully theirs, well then, so much the better. Just so long as Frank Shards paid anyway.

They got their ninety head cut out at last, even though it took near to three hours. The men were so wet, by then, that they had ceased to trouble about it, except to be dimly aware of the damp chill creeping into their very bones. They held the herd to a tight bunch. Jesse and Bill Rust doing the double chore of riding point and flank, Yerby and Lee pushing the drag.

The river crossing was the worst part, the steers balking like stubborn mules until Kells came up and whipped the leaders into control. It was almost, Yerby considered, as though Kells pitted his whole personality against the small brains of these ornery creatures; forced them to obey him by the sheer weight of his will-power. It was a fanciful thought for Yerby and he grinned to himself as he pushed on the drag-herd and occasionally dipped his head so that the rain water could trickle away out of the wide hat-brim.

If there had been little talk before, there was still less on this return journey.

Once Kells rode up to Jesse on the left flank.

'You got a fenced pasture you can shove this lot in, Jess?'

The youngster nodded. 'Fence ain't so good in places but I reckon it'll hold up for a few days.'

'We'll have to start in on changing those brands at the first light.'

'You figure Arrow–?'

Kells interrupted. 'Apart from Arrow, sooner those brands are changed and healed over, sooner you can get rid of some of the beef for cash.'

Jesse wondered why he hadn't thought of that, until he realised his whole mind and being had been tense with anxiety over this thing. Fear of a big spread like Arrow, with its ruthless owner, he reflected, did not die in a night...

It was approaching dawn before the small herd had been settled safely in the big fenced pasture a mile to the east. The men returned to the cabin, cold, wet and dispirited. Yet something had been achieved of which each one might feel justly proud. It had been almost too easy, Kells thought and yet – why not? They had not been expected and Frank was still probably biting his nails about Kells and Zip Cantrell.

They made whatever dry changes of clothes they could, while Bill stoked up the stove and in between hashing up a hot meal, draped wet garments near to the fire, spreading them on saw-horses and wooden boxes.

At five o'clock they sat down to an appetizing meal of bacon, beans, flapjacks and coffee. The food as plain, but it was piping hot and there was plenty of it and as bellies were filled and the cold evaporated from their bones, they began to feel that glow of satisfaction which had been washed from them by the night's chill rain.

'Well we got our beef and we got the rain,' Bill Rust said refilling coffee mugs. 'Reckon the Rust brothers owe a debt to Lee and Bill, here.'

Jesse said. 'That's right enough. You shore got our thanks, Lee. You too, Bill. You figger those tracks'll be washed clean away?'

Kells shook his head slowly. 'I doubt it. The rain wasn't torrential though it soaked us all right.'

Bill glanced at his brother. 'That means Arrow's goin' to be at us before long.'

Lee regarded the younger brother almost incuriously. 'That's a safe bet, Bill. Even if the tracks don't show up, Frank Shane will figure what's happened.'

'How can he?'

'He'll probe every possibility and come to the inevitable conclusion,' Kells said quietly. 'Frank Shane's nobody's fool and I didn't figure we'd fool him over this. Reckon you knew that if you got your cattle back there'd have to be a showdown with Arrow, sooner or later.'

Bill said, 'Yes,' but his tone was edged with a kind of faint surprise.

Marion Starr glanced up from the stack of dishes in the kitchen sink as her ears caught the unfamiliar footfalls across the board floor.

'Why, Anna!' she exclaimed with obvious delight. 'This is a pleasant surprise even if it does sound kind of–' Marion broke off as she took in Anna's white face; the drawn look about the mouth and eyes.

'Sit down, my dear, and I'll fix you some coffee. You look like you've seen a ghost. What's happened?'

Anna Collier sank down into the rocker near the table, grateful for its hard support. She was dressed for riding and her clothes bore traces of dust in spite of the settling rain of last night.

Lettie was busy at the stove and between dealing with stacks of dishes, Marion was helping with the cooking.

'Looks like I ought to be helping you,

Marion,' Anna said with a faint smile. 'Gil off to-day?'

'Not only off to-day but probably will be, permanently, by next week. He's been offered a good job at Dell's Deck. He doesn't really want to quit but–' Marion brought the now heated coffee across to the table, poured out two cupfuls and pushed one across to Anna together with a bowl of sugar.

Anna nodded. 'Sure I know. Gil had an easy job here but you couldn't afford to compete with Dell's when it came to wages.'

Marion nodded and sat down. 'That's just it, Anna. You know we don't make all that much out of this place.'

'Listen, Marion.' Anna leaned forward across the table. 'I know you're only talking to give me time to think. Well, I guess I've already thought about one thing at any rate. I've quit Arrow for good. Frank's a murderer–'

'I know, dear. Kells has been here. He told me how Cantrell came to the line-cabin to kill him with Frank's sanction and how you warned him and Bill Yerby. Don't worry. I'm the only one he's told. I've been terribly worried about you, Anna. Oh, I'm so glad you've decided to get away from that crew of gunmen. You'll stay with me and Lettie, of course, for as long as you want.'

Anna smiled. 'I've just been thinking Marion. About Gil, I mean. If you had room for me here – could put up with me – I could help with the cooking, do Gil's work – just for my keep, I mean, of course. I don't want wages.'

Marion said eagerly. 'Why, that's fine, Anna. Wonderful! Of course you can stay and help us. It sounds like a marvellous solution to both our problems. Now, what's going to happen about Arrow and Kells, do you know?'

Anna shrugged as she sipped the coffee gratefully. 'Maybe you know more than I do. I haven't even seen Lee Kells since I left the line-cabin. Is he all right?'

Marion nodded. 'He was in here early last night. He met the Rust brothers. You know–?'

Anna said. 'Sure I know.' Her eyes were bitter. 'Frank's been robbing them for weeks, a little at a time. Figures to drive them out that way. Not that he ever told me, but I've seen it all going on and tried to turn a blind eye, to make excuses for him. You see, dear,' Anna finished almost desperately, 'it was the only home I had–'

'You have another one now,' the other woman put in quietly, 'and you can quit worrying.'

'What about Bill Yerby?' Anna asked.

'He's all right. Lee was meeting him later. I think Bill was joining up with Lee to help the Rust brothers.'

'Help them? What way? I heard a rumour

190

they were quitting the valley.'

Marion understood. For several months now Anna had been in love with the dark-haired Jesse Rust, even though they had only met once or twice in town. And all along, Anna Collier had felt a strong sense of guilt with herself. Whilst she lived at Frank Shane's big ranch and accepted his food and lodging, Frank's men were out nights robbing Jesse and his brother in order to drive them out and so spread Arrow's herd across Clayton's strip.

'What do you think they'll do, Marion?'

'Knowing Kells as I do, for all that he's a stranger to Creation Valley and Lordville, he'll get Yerby and the Rust boys to fight back.'

'There'll be gun-play and bloodshed,' Anna said almost to herself. 'I could have hoped that Frank had succeeded in driving them out. At least Jesse and Bill would have their lives. Now perhaps they'll be killed for a handful of cattle.'

'Not for a handful of cattle, Anna. If there's a fight and I guess that's inevitable, it'll be for the right to defend their own home and range and stock. Lee's giving them the chance to do that because it fits in with his plans to fight Frank. What sort of a man would you think Jesse was if he ran out in the face of Lee's and Yerby's help?'

'Better a live coward than a dead hero,'

Anna murmured.

'Do you really believe that?'

'No, I guess not. I–' She rose abruptly. 'We can talk about this later. Right now, Lettie wants some help. Give me an apron, Marion...'

Frank Shane stood in the ranch yard, listening to Phil Dukes and as the Arrow rider told his story, Shane felt a bitter fury ride him and anger left its dark revealing stain on his leathery cheeks.

Earlier that day, Phil Dukes had been riding a hog-back about a mile or two away from the bedded down trail-herd. He had glanced at the tiny shape of the line-shack and then turned away vaguely puzzled over something he could not quite define.

He neck-reined his mount a few moments later and returned his gaze to the line-cabin. There was an air, almost of desolation about the place and it took Phil Dukes a full three minutes before he realised it was mainly on account of the absence of any smoke from the shack. Phil knew that a fire would be going for coffee and later to heat a midday meal for Denkern and Sol Schultz. It was unlikely that they would let the stove out and Phil knew that in the clear morning air, even at that distance he should be able to see a thin column of smoke, however illusive, in the clear, rain-washed air.

He thought about this for a few moments, noting now that the herd was milling about more than usual, an in any case, by rights, Flip and Sol should be out there on the range, soothing the cattle and holding them in a tight bunch.

Dukes put his horse to the steep down grade from the hog-back, negotiating the rough slope with all the skill of a born horseman.

It took him a half-hour to descend to the flat ground and another twenty minutes to reach the shack.

Close to, he didn't like the look of things at all. The door was shut.

Phil slid from leather and ground-tied his pony. He eased the six-gun in its holster and called out sharply.

'Flip! Sol! You inside there?'

A muffled grunt sounded dimly from inside, followed by a series of thuds. Then, before Dukes could move forward, the door swung slowly open. Flip was lying full-length on the ground, a bandana half around his chin, his ankles tied together. In that brief moment of surprise, Dukes realised that Denkern had been bound and gagged, probably all night, and had only recently managed to get his hands free. Hearing Dukes, he had left the chore of attacking the rope round his boots and had half crawled, half dragged himself to the door.

Now Phil leaped forward, untying the bandana with difficulty and then, unable to loosen the knots in the rope, he drew his knife and hacked the bonds to pieces.

'Christ!' Denkern said in a hoarse voice, 'Am I glad to see you, Phil!'

Dukes went on inside, while Flip slowly massaged his arms and legs and flexed his stiff muscles.

Sol Schultz had also managed partly to remove the bandana gag from his mouth but had been able to do little to get his hands free.

'The pilgrim who tied you up,' Dukes muttered, severing the ropes with his knife, 'sure knew how to tie knots. Who was it, Flip?'

Denkern had come to stand over Schultz while the latter tried to regain his circulation. Then Flip shoved open a window tying back the gunny sack curtain. Dukes turned out the still burning lamp and set fire to the wood in the stove.

The coffee-pot was on top and while the wood caught, Denkern and Schultz told their story.

Dukes listened attentively and at last, satisfied that neither were the worse for being trussed up half the night, mounted his horse and rode back with all speed to the ranch...

'Did they catch a good look at this bustard who jumped them, Phil?' Frank demanded.

Dukes said. 'He was masked, Frank, like I

told you. Hat well over his eyes. Flip said he kept away from the lamp. But it was all over in a few minutes. Schultz tried for him after he'd pistol-whipped Flip, but the stranger was too quick for Sol. They figgered they must've stayed "out" for a couple of hours or so. Rest of the time until I arrived they'd been having one hell of a time with those ropes.'

Frank said. 'What about the herd? Is it all right?' and Dukes cursed fluently realising that in his haste to report back he had scarcely given the herd a second glance.

Shane could see what had happened and his face was ugly with anger. 'Why else should they have trussed up Denkern and Schultz if it wasn't to steal some of the cattle?'

Dukes shifted uncomfortably. 'Reckon I oughta thought of that, Frank. 'Course the boys didn't hear nothin', seein' as they were "out" for a couple hours or more.'

Frank cursed softly. 'Hasn't anyone any idea who jumped them?'

Phil Dukes paused. He had rather taken a shine to that fellow, Lee Kells, but Dukes was a man who gave his loyalty to the one who paid him, whatever the rights or wrongs of the thing. Too bad about Kells, he thought.

'I've only seen knots tied like that once before, Frank,' Phil went on. 'They was done by Lee Kells.'

'Kells!' Frank spat the name with all the

venom at his command. 'I might've known that bustard was behind this. He's been behind everything bad that's happened to Arrow. Where's Cal?' Frank demanded.

'Saw him over to the corrals when I came bustin' in,' Dukes said.

'Get him for me, Phil,' Frank said, turning back to the house.

He mounted the gallery steps and crossed to where Schillinger sat in a cushioned rocker, his left arm splinted in a sling.

Schillinger had insisted on coming down and running things from the gallery. The news about Zip had seemed to strengthen him and like Frank, George Schillinger's whole soul burned with hatred towards Lee Kells.

Schillinger had heard most of the conversation from where he had sat and now his glittering black eyes were turned questioningly on Frank's face.

'I've sent for Cal,' Shane told his ramrod. 'He's filling Zip's place.'

'What you goin' to do, Frank?'

Shane breathed deeply. 'We'll get that herd to Hide City, George; Cal Beston will be in charge and he'll have to make do with fewer riders.

'When the beef's delivered and paid for, I'm getting Cal to round up some more riders in Hide City.'

'You don't know for sure any beef's been

rustled, Frank,' George said. 'And, if so, who in hell would try it?'

Shane's eyes glittered. His big hands were bunched into fists and a pulse throbbed in his thick neck.

'By God, George. Kells is behind this all right, make no mistake. We'll find out how many cows have gone and where they trailed them to. Then we'll comb the range and smash Lee Kells once and for all.'

'He couldn't have done this alone,' Schillinger said presently.

'I'd thought of that, George. I've been trying to figure who Kells could have tied in with. There's only one answer as I see it.'

'Who?'

'Those goddamned rawhiders!' Frank gritted savagely. 'If that's so, we'll smoke them out with hot lead when the boys come back from Hide City.'

Chapter Thirteen

A CONVERSATION OVERHEARD

The Rust boys, after the reaction of that dismal dawn, were jubilant at what had been achieved, thanks to Kells, with such comparative ease. But Lee, helping them with the branding, warned them that the thing was by no means finished.

As Lee had figured, Jesse had experienced no difficulty in producing a running-iron and over a red-hot fire, kept at a high temperature, Lee hammered and bent the angled end of the iron to the size and pattern he required.

The first try was not completely successful, but Lee made some adjustments and after another steer had been thrown and tied in the big, fenced meadow, he carefully applied the hot iron to the existing Arrow brand.

This Arrow stuff had only recently been rounded up and branded; the burns were fresh and not yet properly healed and this made the task of superimposing the contour of the oak-leaf simpler and less obvious.

Even then, Kells knew that a discerning eye, looking for a changed brand, would spot it, but that was not the point. He was guessing now that already Frank would have made something of the few visible tracks and would be smart enough to have deduced that the ninety cows had been hazed across the river into Clayton's Strip. It was just a question of time, Lee thought grimly, before Frank brought his riders over to clean up Oak-leaf.

Thus, the main idea for changing the Arrow brand to Oak-leaf, was to enable Jesse and Bill to sell some of the cows late summer or early fall. By that time Lee reckoned that the changed brands would pass muster with any buyer and be accepted without question as Oak-leaf.

Once Kells had mastered the knack of this branding, and satisfied that the result was passably good, he passed the job over to Jesse and Bill Rust.

After one or two false starts, Jesse got the hang of it then it was a question merely of throwing and hog-tying each steer with one man to hold down the kicking hind-quarters, the other man to apply the hot iron.

Lee pointed to a high ridge on the range, a few miles away.

'I'm taking a look-see from that point,' he told them. 'You coming, Bill?'

Yerby nodded and began cinching his own and Lee's rig. They mounted and Kells called, 'Keep an eye open and your carbines handy.'

Jesse, sweaty but cheerful looked up and nodded. He pointed to the two Winchesters on the ground, alongside their canteens and bedrolls and grinned, and Bill Rust waved a hand as Lee put his horse towards the ridge at a long loping run, followed by Yerby.

This high point was steeper than it had appeared from a distance, so that they were forced to tie their mounts to a tree and negotiate the ridge on foot.

Kells brought a pair of Army field glasses with him and on reaching the summit, squatted down and began his careful survey of the country.

He remained hunkered down for a long while, occasionally raking the country through the glasses and, in between, smoking cigarettes and talking to Yerby.

Bill said, presently, 'I could eat some of that grub in the saddle-bags and I sure could use some of that whisky.'

Lee nodded and Yerby scrambled back down the ridge to the tethered horses below.

He was back within fifteen minutes, his arms full of saddle-bags. He dropped them on to the ground, but carefully, remembering in time the glass bottle, and unslung a canteen from his shoulders. He wiped sweat from his face and Lee, making his periodic survey of the country, said, 'There they go, Bill. Take a look.'

Yerby took the glasses and focused them on the distant smudge of rising dust.

The picture seen by the naked eye as a chalk smudge on the horizon, became clearly etched and detailed in front of the powerful lenses.

'That's Arrow's trail-herd, all right,' Bill confirmed presently. 'Reckon they've got every gosh-darn man along with 'em too.'

'How many you make, Bill?'

Yerby counted slowly, though even with the glasses it was not only impossible to identify the riders individually, but difficult enough to pick them out amid the moving, dust-raising herd.

'Eight, I reckon, Lee,' Yerby said at last. 'There's a thick cloud of dust at the drag and I cain't quite figure whether there's two or three riders in back.' He handed the glasses back and Lee held them steady a long moment.

'Eight I make it too,' he said slowly. He lowered the glasses and looked at the other man. 'By God, Bill. Then Frank's going along too, unless the last man is Curly, the cook.'

Yerby shook his head slowly. 'Curly don't as a rule go when it's a short trail-drive like Hide City. The boys muck in with the cookin'; they ain't that along on the trail, anyway, and they kin allus fill up with food and liquor at Hide City.'

Bill Yerby's glance came across and rested on Kells' bleak face.

'You was figgerin' on bracin' Frank at the ranch. Now it looks like you'll haveta wait 'till he gets back. Maybe,' Bill added grimly, 'he'll be bracin' us.'

'I'll go over and make sure,' Lee said, 'that it's Curly who's stayed behind and not Frank. After that we've got less than a week to turn Oak-leaf into a fort.'

'About that,' Yerby nodded. 'They know the Hide City trail blindfold and kin push them dogies along twen'y, twen'y-five miles a day.

'Three days to get there, two days to get

201

blind, and back the next day.'

Yerby began rummaging for food in the saddle-bags, producing a can of beans and some soda crackers as well as the whisky.

They ate hungrily, Bill washing his meal down with rye, and Lee, at this time of day, preferring canteen water, even luke-warm.

Yerby collected the scrubbed tin plates, replacing them in the saddle-bags. Kells said, 'Let's get back, Bill, and see how the branding's going.'

Yerby nodded as they turned and descended the ridge to the waiting horses. For a moment they watched the slow-moving dust cloud on the horizon as it swung northwards at a snail's pace; then, with one accord they shook up their mounts, pointing them back towards Oak-leaf's fenced meadow.

Lea Franchot sat at the dressing table in her room above the Silver Dollar and gazed deeply into the worn gilt mirror as she combed and brushed her thick black hair.

There was no need to hurry to-day; no need to paint herself even, or don the hard veneer which was as much her stock-in-trade as the shoulderless revealing dresses she wore during 'business' hours.

Art was out of town and she could relax for a day and think of other things. Lee Kells, for example.

She put down the brush and gazed searchingly, objectively, at her reflection in the mirror and almost disinterestedly observed the long hair as shining black as a raven's wing. She caught herself frowning, drawing the dark brows together, so that a hard line furrowed the smooth surface of her skin. The smoky grey eyes probed deeper still as though by sheer concentration she could discover truths which lay way back and beyond the image in the glass.

Is it possible for a woman to change back after a life of this? she thought and knew with a bitter certainly that such a thing did not happen in a thousand years.

Since she had met the stranger, Lee Kells; had risked her job and perhaps her life in staking him on a sudden whim; since she had felt his arms around her and his mouth hard-pressed against her searching lips, that night beside the bubbling creek, since then Angelea Franchot had contrived to do what so many women had essayed and failed. The leopard cannot change its spots, she had told herself a dozen times over, not even for love.

What she had told Kells that night had been nothing more nor less than the truth. There was no room for a woman without kith or kin in a western community unless she could cook, or sew, or teach or – attract custom to a honky-tonk! And in the minds of the people who dwelt in cow-towns and frontier settlements, there were no finer degrees of shading when it came to assessing the womenfolk. There were the good and the bad, just like that. No in-betweens, no good 'bad' women and no bad 'good' ones.

There was a sharp dividing line between good and bad, loose and moral, a hard-drawn line as strong and as substantial as any high close-boarded fence, even though it existed only in the minds of these self-appointed judges of a community's moral standards.

Even as Lea fought to find a way round this, she knew the utter futility of it, just as though she were beating her lovely head against a physical wall...

Presently with a deep sigh that was nearly a sob, she threw down the brush and began braiding her hair, remembering the style which she'd employed years ago. The change amazed her, softening the contours of her face as it did. Next she took cream from a pot and smeared her face, removing all traces of cosmetics with a cloth. This operation brought a faint colour to Lea's normally pale cheeks, and she was quick and pleased to notice that her skin was still flawless in spite of the life she had been compelled to live.

She slipped the wrapper from her shoulders and shrugged into the blouse and divided skirt previously taken from the big trunk.

It had been a long time since Angelea Franchot had done any riding. To-day she felt an irresistible urge to climb into leather and fork a horse across the range; to feel the wind tugging at her hair and whipping her face and body...

W.O. Sellars glanced up from his seat in the open doorway of his office. He saw the girl and for a moment was hard put to place her.

She stood on the runway, looking at him, a half-smile playing on her face.

'Lea!' the old man said. 'By God, you do look different. Like you was–'

'Like I was a lady?' Lea said with a bitter twist to her mouth.

W.O. shifted his vast weight uncomfortably and flushed as a man will when a woman reads his mind without effort.

Sellars scratched his head and then, realising that Lea Franchot was dressed for riding, lumbered to his feet and crossed over to her side.

'You figgerin' on ridin' some place, girlie?' he said.

She nodded and shrugged. 'Some place, any place, just so long as I can grab me a handful of fresh air and forget the Silver Dollar for a few hours.'

Sellars nodded his silent understanding. 'I'll go saddle a mount for you.'

Shortly, Lea mounted the fresh buckskin, swinging astride its back easily on account of the freedom rendered by the divided skirt.

The buckskin was eager for exercise and once out of town Lea found it easier to give the animal its head. She was a born horse-woman and in spite of a long absence from the saddle retained her seat with ease.

Her hair so carefully pinned, less than an hour ago, was loose now and flying before the wind like the buckskin's silvery mane and tail. But she didn't care. There was no one to see her and she knew, even if there were, she still would not care. She had a feeling of a bird suddenly released from its cage, finding a spiritual as well as a physical ecstasy in flying through the morning air.

She reined in to give both herself and her mount a blow and after a rest set the buckskin galloping again for the sheer delight of the thing.

She smiled to herself, anticipating with a rueful grimace, that to-morrow her seat would be sore! But to-morrow was another day. To-day this very moment she was vib-rantly alive.

She thought again of Kells and it had a sobering effect on her as she put her gaze to the trail, taking in the dust cloud that hung above it a few miles away.

Somehow, the sight of that yellow dust – cattle on the move to Hide City – reminded her again, sharply, of the bleak-faced rider who had come to Hide City looking for a man. Had Kells found his man in Frank Shane of the Arrow spread? She wondered and suddenly shuddered.

Perhaps even now this was an Arrow herd trailing up from the Bend of Creation. This was the trail they always used and there were no other big outfits situated on the bend.

A fierce surge of impatience rode Angelea Franchot then. She held the horse quite still, in her mind urging the moving cattle to a faster gait, so that she could identify the outfit. If this were Arrow, she might learn something. Perhaps to-night she would surprise the other girls and the barkeeps at the Silver Dollar by unexpectedly returning to duty.

She waited there another half-hour while the buckskin impatiently pawed the ground and threw up its head to the jingling accompaniment of bridle-chains.

The slow-moving herd was veering off now to the north-east, she saw. That meant they were driving straight to the loading pens alongside the spur track east of town.

She lifted the reins and shook up the horse, who was eager enough to race again.

Long before the herd had reached the loading pens, Lea was riding towards the outfit like any young lady out for a morning's ride.

Sweating, hard-worked point and flank riders did not allow the handling of the cattle to interfere with such gallantries as doffing sombreros and waving bright scarves with sun-blackened hands.

Lea smiled, acknowledging the greetings and yipees, not because she cared for any of the Arrow hands, but because it was not in her true nature to erect that cold barrier of aloofness which so many 'well-bred' women seemed to consider the hall-mark of being well-bred.

Lea noted with a sudden start, the big, blocky figure of Frank, half-enveloped in the dust of the drag. Did this mean that Frank, after all, was not the one Kells was after or – did it mean that already they had clashed and Frank had emerged the victor?

Lea found herself suddenly trembling. Now that she could no longer side-step the issues; now that she was face to face with something definite, she knew beyond any doubt that her feelings for Lee Kells were such as she had never experienced before. There was a deep bitterness within her now, that this thing had come too late.

Yet, she smiled to herself. Even had it not been so, there had been no indication from Kells himself, that night at the creek, that the incident held any deep significance for him.

The sun had gone out of her day and the previous zest for riding the range was now only a sour after-taste on the palate of her feelings.

Almost dispiritedly, Angelea Franchot pointed the buckskin towards town and presently brought it back to W.O. Sellar's livery.

Hide City was alive once again with its

nightly cacophony of noise and laughter.

Against the background music of the town's night life rose the sharper individual sounds on Main Street itself. The sudden crescendo of men's voices as their owners tromped the board-walks; the soft thud of hoofs in the stirring dust; the rattle of harness and wheel-brakes and the thousand and one personal and prosaic notes which single themselves out from the main orchestration by reason of their very individuality.

A bunch of riders swung their ponies with wild abandon on to Main, narrowly missing vehicles and pedestrians alike. They were yelling, with the wild exuberance of their kind, one-two firing six-guns into the air, causing hitched horses to stir and cavort uneasily at the tie-rails.

A few of the Arrow riders kept going down street. The rest swung their mounts into the rail in front of the Silver Dollar and racked their mounts.

Frank Shane's big blocky figure led the way into the saloon. Cal Beston, Eddie Hindel and Slim Tuckfold were with him and they all had gold pieces in their pockets.

Shane's herd had fetched a good price with the cattle trading company and most of the Arrow riders intended spending their trail-herd bonuses just as fast as they could. But Frank and the three gunsels with him had more important work to do first...

Lea saw them as soon as they came in and somehow sensed that these Arrow hands with Shane were not here entirely for pleasure. She watched them as they bellied up to the bar and drank, not in the carefree fashion of hands fresh off the trail, but with a careful restraint as though taking their pleasures sadly.

Something's going to happen, to-night, Lea thought, as she spun the roulette wheel and flicked the ball in. She watched the game almost automatically, pushing chips across to winners and raking in from the losers.

Presently Frank and one of his men went over to a booth taking their drinks with them. Lea saw the other two slide out of the saloon doors quietly and unobtrusively.

Jack Fallow, a thin-faced house gambler, sat alone at a baize-covered table idly trying to cheat himself at a game of solitaire. He caught Lea's eye and swept the cards together with practised ease. He walked over to the roulette table.

'I feel like a drink and a sit-down, Jack. Would you take over for me?' The look he gave her was answer enough. There was little, if anything, that Jack Fallow would not do for Angelea Franchot except perhaps, cross-up Art Lucas.

'Sure, honey,' he said in that soft-as-silk voice of his and Lea smiled and threw him a grateful glance.

Kirk the barkeep grinned at her. 'Usual coloured water, Lea, or something stronger?'

'Something stronger, Kirk. I feel tired.'

'You shouldn't a' come back to-night. You ain't had a day off in weeks.'

Lea shrugged her bare shoulders.

'The hell with it! What's there to do; where's to go?'

Kirk produced a shot glass full of whisky and leaned across the bar.

'I could think of things to do if we both had the same day off.'

She smiled. 'You stick to your knitting, Kirk,' she said picking up the drink and moving away in an apparently aimless fashion.

She had noted the booth in which Shane and his riders had ensconced themselves and hoped that the seat on the opposite side was vacant. It was, and Lea slid her legs in under the table and placed the untouched glass on the boards. She leaned back against the thin partition, her eyes closed, for all the world a picture of a tired woman resting quietly.

'How many men you figure you'll want them to pick up, boss?' the man behind was saying.

'Four at least, Cal,' Frank Shane's voice came through the flimsy barrier clearly enough, even though the words were softly uttered.

She remembered the man now, the one whom Frank had called Cal. Cal Beston it

211

was, she thought, and like Cantrell and one-two others she had met on previous occasions, he was a killer, she knew.

'After we get back,' Shane's voice went on quietly, 'we'll ride down to Clayton's Strip and wipe out them damned rawhiders along with Kells, dam' his soul to hell!'

Lea's whole body stiffened though she still kept her eyes closed. Presently she reached for the shot glass and sipped at the contents.

She had not expected to hear anything quite so definite nor had she figured to have heard it so soon. It had been no more than a hunch on her part, that, by the very restrained actions of these men, they were preparing some sort of plan...

She heard feet shuffle in the booth in back of her and wondered if the conference had been broken up already. But one of them returned in a few minutes with fresh drinks. She strained her ears to catch any further conversation. It was getting more difficult now with the increasing amount of noise in the saloon and at the farther end the girls were dancing with some of the customers to the tinny strains of a piano...

The whisky glass was empty now and suddenly boots shuffled again behind the booth partition, more noisily this time. She dared not risk a look but guessed that other men had joined Frank and Cal Beston.

'This is Lew White, boss,' a man's voice

said, and Lea heard the low-uttered almost surly acknowledgment. 'Slim's comin' in shortly,' the man went on, 'Figgers he's picked up a couple of hands as can earn some extra *dinero*.'

Frank Shane grunted and again, as before, came sounds of a further interruption. An exchange of names, hoarsely spoken; a quiet interchange of viewpoints including a suggested amount of money.

'It's fifty a month,' Frank Shane said, 'And bonuses for – other work.'

A cold trickle of fear ran down Lea's spine as she read into these quietly uttered words, a hidden and deadly significance. Her mind was in a whirl. She had no idea of what had been happening in the Bend of Creation. All she could tell at the moment from this overheard conversation was that Kells was still alive, presumably on a place called Clayton's Strip and with someone to whom Frank Shane had referred as dam' rawhiders. It seemed obvious too that Shane was without question the man Kells had been looking for, and, Shane knew all about Lee Kells.

He was hiring gun-hands at this very moment, so that, once back to Arrow, they could start in and clean up this place on Clayton's Strip and kill Lee along with his friends.

Lea's heart was pounding so loudly that for a few moments the sound of it seemed to drown all other noises.

At last she moved, quietly and casually returning to the bar with her empty glass. As she paused she threw a quick glance at the huddle of men at the table. They were still busy talking in quiet tones and drinking...

Chapter Fourteen

A DAM' CLOSE THING

Inside the dilapidated Oak-leaf ranch house Lee awoke and rolled out of his blanket.

Ranch house was rather a grand name for this drunken-looking building of sun-warped timbers, he thought, as he washed up at the pump in the yard. But though badly in need of repair the building was far from hopeless as a defensive position.

Lee's mind was running on as he towelled himself and combed back the thick black hair. Even if Arrow were away best part of a week, there was not overmuch time to fortify and strengthen the place; equip it, if necessary for a siege and also haze the cattle to some place of comparative safety such as a small hidden canyon in the broken country north.

There would have to be at least one trip to

town for more stores and equipment particularly as the Rust boys were short on anything like a buggy or spring wagon. Supplies had to be put into gunny sacks and loaded over the saddle-horn and Kells had no way of knowing how long the expected fight would last. He did know, with a cold and final certainty, that it would not end until either Oakleaf were all killed or else Frank himself were sent off Clayton's Strip feet first.

It was a moot point whether all the Arrow hands would continue fighting if once Frank were killed.

His ablutions finished, Lee re-entered the house and tramped through to the kitchen. He fed wood to the stove, soaked a screw of old papers in coal-oil and applied a match.

He placed the coffee-pot atop the stove, opened the damper and built himself a smoke, watching through the window the eastern sky change from pale blue and oyster to saffron and cobalt. It still wanted an hour to sunrise.

From the adjoining room he could hear the familiar noises of awakening men, loud yawns, creaking limbs and the soft pad of stockinged feet searching for boots.

He took down a cup from the home-made shelves that did service as a dresser, placed it on the table and inspected the coffee. He waited with a barely suppressed impatience as the java slowly heated.

On a sudden impulse he turned and went through the rear door, heading for the makeshift corral near the house. He gave Red a feed of oats from the grain bin and afterwards quickly saddled and bridled him.

He led the pony round to the front of the house, leaving it ground-haltered near the door. By this time the coffee-pot was bubbling and Bill Yerby was in the kitchen foraging for another cup.

'Howdy, Lee. Cain't you sleep?'

Kells' smile was fleeting. 'Figure on going into town, Bill. We could use some more cans of food and a few more boxes of .44–.40 shells.'

Bill nodded and grabbed the coffee-pot handle with his kerchief, before sloshing the thick liquid into the cups. He added sweetening from a bowl on the table. 'Want for me to come, Lee?'

Kells shook his head. 'I'd rather you stay with the Rust boys and keep an eye on things. See if you can find some fence-posts and timber to make good these windows. I'll fetch back some nails and bob-wire.'

'Bob-wire! What the hell!'

Kells said, 'I'm going to Arrow to find out whether Frank really has gone on this trail-drive to Hide City. If he hasn't, if he's still back at Arrow, there won't be any need for all these precautions, 'less I'm damned unlucky and get hit first.'

'But bob-wire! You fixin' to fence us in?'

Lee nodded. 'Just around the house, at a distance of, say, twenty-thirty yards. It'll mean sweating some to sink posts but we should have nearly a week.'

Yerby nodded. 'I begin to see, Lee. That don't sound like a bad idea. If Frank attacks as he sure will, the fence'll stop them rushing us.'

'Even more than that, Bill,' Kells said finishing the cup of coffee. 'It might just keep them from burning us out.'

Lee skipped breakfast and took out for Lordville. His first call was to Race Arnold's office.

The lawman toed a chair from the wall indicating it for Lee, and sank into the swivel-chair at his desk.

'What's doin', Kells?'

Lee said, 'Arrow's making their trail-drive as per schedule to Hide City.'

'Right. Saw the dust-cloud myself yesterday.'

'You don't know, then, whether Frank himself was trail-boss?'

Race Arnold's grey head moved slowly from side to side.

'Couldn't say, but the way you've whittled down his crew, so far, wouldn't surprise me none if Frank was with them.

'You asked me to sit tight,' Arnold went on, 'an' I been doin' just that. But there's goin' to be trouble I reckon when Frank gets back.'

'There'll be trouble all right,' Kells agreed grimly, 'but I don't figure it'll be your grief, Sheriff. This is between Shane and me.'

'That's alright, Kells,' Arnold said, 'but supposin'–' He flushed and bit his lip.

Lee smiled thinly. 'Supposing Frank kills me? Is that what you were going to say? Well, he might, Race, at that. But I promise you I'll take him with me. Whatever the outcome of this, Frank Shards is going to pay.'

Arnold's face was worried. 'Don't figger I ought to be lettin' you take the law into your own hands, Kells. 'Sides which I got so I don't know which side o' the fence I'm supposed to be.'

'We've hazed back the Oak-leaf cattle that Arrow rustled. It's no secret, I guess. Frank will have figured that one out, easily. When he comes back – if he's gone to Hide City – it won't be me taking the law into my own hands, it'll be Arrow and its hired gun-hands.'

The sheriff tried a new tack. 'You figger you can stand up to a dozen or so gun-slingers, you and Yerby and those two kids?'

Lee rose. 'You'll see, Sheriff.'

He moved towards the door and suddenly turned back. 'You handled cattle much, Arnold? Reckon you have, though, judging by your hands.'

Arnold nodded. 'I've been a lawman only six years, Kells, since about when Frank–, well you can guess that part of it.

'Before then I worked cattle for thirty years, with various spreads. Why?'

'I was thinking of your wife and kids and the extra money you need. This sheriffing doesn't seem hardly a full-time job, particularly if Arrow's broken up and those gunnies sent packing.'

'I don't get it. What's the breaking up of Arrow got to do with me except lose me that "extra" *dinero?*'

'Only this,' Kells said slowly. 'I've made a few enquiries and as far as I know, Frank Shards' next-of-kin is – Anna Collier.'

'I reckon that's likely. What of it?'

'With Frank out of the way and the old Arrow hands dealt with, Anna Collier would want a good foreman-manager, wouldn't she?'

Before Arnold could answer, Kells had turned and tramped out of the office.

It was still not yet nine o'clock when Lee entered Starr's Restaurant and hauled up abruptly at sight of Anna Collier carrying a tray of food from the counter to a table.

He gave a low whistle of surprise as Anna threw him a quick smile. She dumped the dishes on to the table and hurried over to the wall table which Lee had chosen.

'What can I get you, sir?' she demanded in

a pseudo business-like voice.

Kells grinned. 'How long has this been going on, Anna?'

'Since the day after I warned you about – you know. I couldn't stand it any longer, Lee. Frank's changed a lot over the past week or so.'

'Ever since I showed up,' Lee said grimly.

She nodded. 'I was scared when I got back from the line-cabin. He tackled me about it. I lied, of course, but he was suspicious. I was really scared, Lee. I stayed awake all that night, or what was left of it, and decided to quit Arrow altogether.

'There isn't much more except that Marion's help, you know, Gil Rabjohn, was leaving. Marion offered me a home here and I figured the best thing I could do was to accept and sort of help out.'

Kells nodded. 'I'm glad you've quit, Anna. There's going to be a deal of powder-smoke in Creation Valley, before long.'

It was not the words themselves, but the way they were spoken and the cold expression in Kells' eyes which caused Anna Collier to shiver and see, in her mind's eye, the sprawled shapes of men with smoking guns clenched in their stiffening hands.

She pushed the images from her and smiled quickly. 'I'll get Marion to fix you some breakfast.'

Kells pushed back his empty plate and

built a cigarette, exploding a match along the edge of the chair. He pushed the chair back by straightening his legs and strolled into the kitchen.

Marion looked up from the stove, her face flushed, a bright smile in her eyes and on her lips.

'Heard you were here, Lee. It's nice to see you again. Was the breakfast all right?'

'Right as rain, thanks. How you making out?'

She wiped flour-covered hands on her apron, gave one last look at the baking and straightened up.

'We're doing all right, Lee. How about you?'

'I'll tell you better when I've met up with Frank.'

'You're still siding the Rust boys?'

He nodded. 'Me and Yerby together. I'm going to Arrow now.'

Her eyes widened in alarm as Anna came back into the kitchen with an empty tray. 'That's taken care of all the late breakfasts, Marion.'

She saw the worry in Marion Starr's eyes and Lee said gently, 'Marion doesn't like the idea of my going to Arrow.'

Marion began to pour coffee for the three of them; Lettie bobbed in from time to time to stack the dirty dishes in the sink.

'It's something that's got to come, Marion,'

Anna said with a new-born philosophy. She turned to Kells as though reading his thoughts. 'I don't know whether Frank's there or not. I left before the trail-drive.' She hesitated for a moment and then added. 'Remember me to Jesse – Jesse Rust, Lee, will you?'

It was Kells' turn to show surprised interest as he got up to go. 'Sure I will, Anna, and the best of luck. *Adios.*'

He went straight from the restaurant to Lordville's hardware shop and purchased half a dozen boxes of Winchester shells. From there he tramped down-street to Joe Ward's Mercantile.

Ward himself waited on Lee and put up the order.

Ward said softly. 'Heerd tell, Mr Kells, that you and Bill Yerby's backin' the Rust boys back on Clayton's Strip.'

Kells said. 'There might be some truth in that, Ward. 'What's your interest?'

'Me,' Joe Ward said. 'I mind my own business as a general rule, but I'm sidin' anyone that's got the guts to buck Arrow. Them riders is a dad-blasted nuisance at times, too. Busted my plate-glass window a coupla times and refused to pay.'

Kells nodded and paid for the stores now packed in two gunny sacks.

'Say,' Ward suggested. 'You don't wanta carry them on your saddle and you sure cain't manage that bob-wire. I'll send Henry with the spring-wagon if you want.'

'That's fine,' Kells had been wondering how to get the coils of wire back to Oak-leaf, 'and you tell Henry to keep his mouth shut about anything he sees out on Clayton's Strip, *sabe?*'

Joe Ward's head nodded vigorously. 'I savvy, Mr Kells. Don't you worry.'

Lee rode slowly towards Creation River and not for the first time in the last ten years, he began to feel a deep and overpowering impatience.

He went over in his mind the events that had shaped themselves since he had first hit Lordville, trying to figure how else he could have played this. Perhaps if he had acted differently; tackled Shards in the first place, he could have saved himself this grim waiting. Perhaps, by now, it would have been all over, one way or the other.

But there had been one good thing come out of this business of playing the thing carefully. Two things, Kells reminded himself.

Firstly he had found allies in the shape of Yerby, the Rust brothers and Anna Collier and secondly, as things had now worked out, Anna had voluntarily quit Arrow. Frank was reverting to type and the bold veneer of bluff bonhomie was wearing thin enough for Anna Collier to see beneath it.

Now Anna had found a home with her friend and was probably happier than she had been when living in the shadow of Frank Shard's uncertain temper.

And Kells quietly and objectively recognised that had he gone to Arrow single-handed, like a mad bull, he himself undoubtedly would have been killed, perhaps leaving Frank alive and unpunished for the terrible crime he had committed in the San Saba Valley.

Now Lee thought, things were evened up a little. There were four men including himself representing Oak-leaf, and unless Frank took on some new riders quickly, the odds were no worse than many a small outfit had faced successfully.

Thinking about the crew, Kells suddenly remembered Schillinger. Schillinger would be at the ranch house together with the oldster, Verne, the ranch servant and handyman! True, Schillinger still had a busted arm, but it was his left arm.

Lee shook up the pony as he made a mental note to watch out for the crafty Schillinger. Once before George had tried to down him with a rigged play. He might try again. Who else might be there? Kells wondered and remembered Curly the cook.

As he rode across the sage-brush dotted range towards the distant cluster of buildings, Lee withdrew the Colt from its holster, checking the loads and testing the breech mechanism.

He came into the yard some time around noon, noting the abandoned-looking air that always clings to buildings devoid of occupants. Yet, Kells was not at all sure the place was as utterly deserted as it seemed.

He stepped out of the saddle, ground-haltering the pony and began his methodical search, heading first for the bunkhouse.

There was no smoke coming from the chimney and yet, if Schillinger were here, somewhere about, surely Curly would have remained behind to cook for him.

Lee entered the bunkhouse, finding evidences of a recent meal. He touched the stove and felt the warmth from a recent fire. Buzz flies crawled over a stack of unwashed dishes on the table. The adjoining cook-shack bore similar indications of recent meals, but there was no sign of Curly or anyone else.

Lee left the bunkhouse and gave the stables and barns his attention. A few ponies were in the stalls and now, outside, Kells could see a distant figure on a horse. The smallness of that figure and the stoop-shouldered contour told Lee that the rider was Verne out on some mysterious errand of his own. Perhaps Schillinger or Curly, if either of them were here, had told him to rope and butcher a steer.

The only occupant of the big corral was

the steel-dust mare. She looked almost as though she had remained there, without attention, since the day Kells had taken the starch out of her.

He moved across to the pole fence and spoke softly. Steel-dust pricked up her ears, whinnied softly and then began to move towards the fence with a half-suspicious reluctance.

For a moment Kells forgot where he was. The bitterness of his ten-year search had somehow never erased his deep fondness for horses. He spoke again, murmuring the commonplace expressions that a man uses to an intelligent animal. It was never the words themselves that counted, only the intimate and soothing cadence of voice and tone.

She was up to the fence now, poking her muzzle over the top and blowing softly down her nostrils. Kells stroked the silky muzzle as the mare scented and recognised her old friend.

Suddenly Kells froze, his whole body stiffening. He dared not move as he heard the footsteps shuffling towards him, for he sensed the gun behind him, trained on his back.

'All right, Kells!' Schillinger's voice was thin with hatred. 'You can turn around, easy though, so I can see how you take it. Move those hands down and you'll get it straight in the back, low down.'

Lee turned slowly, keeping both hands at shoulder height. His back was now to the fence, the steel-dust watching the proceedings with nervous uncertainty.

Schillinger stood a bare twenty-five yards away and Lee cursed himself softly for having been caught so unawares. Even though, when he had looked at the house, he had felt certain Frank was not there, he should have concerned himself more deeply with Schillinger's probable presence, he told himself bitterly.

'This is it, Kells!' Schillinger said and Lee noted that in spite of the left arm in its sling, George Schillinger held the long-barrelled Colt in a steady rock-like right hand.

'This is the last time you'll come snoopin' around Arrow,' the ex-foreman continued thumbing back the hammer of the gun. 'Well, now, Kells, let's see you beg for mercy, or don't you know how painful it is to die slow with a .45 slug in your guts?'

Kells said, 'Cut out the drama, George. You've got the drop on me. What are you waiting for?'

For a brief moment, the other man seemed slightly taken aback. He had half-expected some plea for mercy, some appeal to his better nature, and here was this bustard Kells inviting him to pull the trigger.

Kells thought, I've got one chance in a thousand if I can do what I did before, on

227

Lordville's Main Street.

He was as tensed now as a coiled spring, his gaze fixed unwinkingly, not on Schillinger's Colt but on the man's deadly, glittering eyes.

He read the change of expression in that black, hate-filled gaze and prepared himself to dive headlong.

Even as the gun roared, the steel-dust's head came up in front of Lee's face, blocking for a split second his vision and obstructing his carefully planned dive.

It took both men a second or two to recover and realise what had happened.

At the crucial moment, the mare had thrust her head over the corral fence, seeking the comforting touch of Kells' hands. Schillinger's gun had roared and the heavy .45 slug had buried itself in the mare's brain.

The legs buckled as she fell heavily against the fence before sliding slowly to the ground. She was dead before she hit the dust and now Lee's gun was out and flaming even as the surprised Schillinger triggered his second shot. But the roar of Schillinger's Colt was but an echo of Lee's gun. It was the same sort of amazing snapshot that Lee had so successfully executed on the drunk in Starr's Restaurant when Race Arnold's life had hung in the balance.

This time, Kells' gun was lifted from the hip in an angle shot. The bullet took Schillinger in the face just below the left eye, channelling a course for itself upwards through the head.

He swayed for a moment on widely-spread legs. The gun slid from his fingers. One half of his face was a mask of blood as he folded up completely and crashed to the ground no more than a second after the steel-dust mare.

Lee slowly wiped the streaming sweat from his face with his shirt-sleeve. He gazed almost stupidly at the smoking gun in his right hand before returning it to its holster. It had been a close thing. A dam' close thing!

Chapter Fifteen

A FRIEND FROM HIDE CITY

For the best part of the next three days Oakleaf toiled at its muscle-aching task.

Under Lee's direction, the fence-posts had been sunk into well-dug holes and gloved hands were already at work with nails and wire-cutters, stretching the lower strands of the wickedly spiked wire from post to post.

Yerby looked at Kells, wiping the sweat from his face. 'I ain't never worked so hard in my life, Lee, and all this for no *dinero*.'

Jesse Rust, stripped to the waist, straightened up from his back-aching task. 'We aim to make this up to both of you,' he said slowly. 'Without Lee and you, Bill, the Rust brothers would be ridin' the chuck-line or tryin' to bum a lift into the next territory.'

Bill Rust nodded his agreement as he worked on the eight-foot, five-bar gate that would, when erected, close the fence in on all encompassing rectangle.

'Talkin' of chuck,' Bill Rust grinned. 'I reckon I'd better knock off and rustle up some supper.'

Kells looked at the lowering sun. 'We've done well, but we've still got another couple of hours yet. Reckon we'll have the two bottom strands fixed all round by dusk.'

When the triangle sounded from the house, aching backs stretched themselves and mask-like faces grinned. The two bottom strands of bob-wire had been fixed from post to post right round the yard. To-morrow would see the work done and to each of them came that brief uplifting mood of satisfaction when the end of a tough chore is in sight.

Sweat-soaked shirts were discarded for clean ones after each man had washed up at the pump in the yard.

Bill had a good meal awaiting them and plates were soon cleaned and cups emptied in short order.

Yerby reached up for a storm-lantern hanging from a hook, 'Got me a busted latigo to

230

fix,' he explained, wiping a match to the wick and dropping the glass back into position.

'Don't set the barns alight,' Lee said.

Yerby grinned and went out into the darkness and Lee said. 'Soon as the fence is finished we must haze the cattle away from the meadow. You got a place in mind, Jesse?'

The elder Rust boy nodded. 'A small canyon not far from here, Lee, and shale and rock most of the way. Plumb difficult for readin' sign. Reckon they'll be safe there.'

'Good. The fence'll keep Arrow well away from the house and they won't be able to get to the cattle. They'll have to fight it out.'

Lee broke off to build a cigarette. Bill Rust was clattering the dishes in the sink.

'Reckon I forgot to give you a message, Jesse. Should have remembered before this.'

'A message? Who from?'

Lee smiled. 'Anna Collier is in town. She's working with Marion Starr in the restaurant.'

'You mean she's quit Arrow?'

Kells nodded, explaining the reasons which had prompted Anna Collier to make her break.

'She said for me to give you her kind regards, Jesse.'

A slow flush stained Jesse's face and his broad lips parted in a pleased grin.

'Reckon I'd no idea she'd ever looked at me, Lee.' There was almost a sheepish expression on his face. 'Guess I've seen her a

coupla times in town and once out ridin'
near the river. That's all.'

Kells sent cigarette smoke down his nostrils. 'When we get out of this jam – if we get
out of it, I'd be calling on Miss Collier, if my
name were Jesse Rust.'

Before the other could think of any suitable
reply, Lee tramped from the room out on to
the night-darkened porch. Dimly, across the
yard he could make out the fence-posts. Here
and there a light, perhaps reflected from the
windows, winked like an isolated star as it
was thrown back from the barbs...

Kells must have dozed out there in the
rocker on the porch. For how long he did
not know. He listened intently for the sound
to repeat itself. The sound that had first
penetrated his sleepy brain. There it was!
The soft hoof-beats of a horse, coming
slowly, hesitantly towards the house.

Silently Kells rose and reached for the six-
gun at his hip. In a moment he had thumbed
back the hammer and had the gun pointed
straight out across the yard. Subconsciously,
he realised he must have slept for some time,
because now the stars were bright and over to
the east the moon's first glow showed in the
indigo sky.

He could make out the dim, almost
ghostly shape of the horse and rider now,
some yards beyond the posts. It was a roan
and white pony, he thought, the white head

232

and stockings showing up against the nebulous background of contrasting colour.

The soft, slow, almost silent approach of this mysterious night rider was almost uncanny and Lee found himself unnaturally tensed as though facing some awful and formidable adversary.

Still the rider came on, as though peering through the night, and, apparently noticing now the beginnings of the bob-wire fence. The pony was halted for a few moments and then, again, urged forward at its former uncertain gait.

There was something vaguely familiar about that small, slim shape atop the horse, and even though it was shrouded in a cloak, still Kells stood there, baffled and puzzled.

The rider came on through the yard until a bare ten yards from the house. Kells heard his name called softly. 'Lee!'

He ran forward then, taking the veranda steps in one jump. He was up to the horse and rider in a matter of seconds, looking up into the fear-filled face of Lea Franchot.

'Lea! What in hell's name–?'

He had no time for more, as with a stifled sob she put out her arms and half fell from the saddle as Kells reached out to hold her.

They stood like that for a moment that was yet immeasurable in finite terms of time. The warmth and softness of her pressed so tightly to him was real and yet chimerical at one and the same time.

'Thank God I've found you, Lee,' she choked. 'I thought I never would. I've been ridin' all over for hours.'

He released her now and smiled down at her. Strangely there was no bitterness in his face at that moment. He patted her shoulders comfortingly.

'Well you've found me now, Lea. Come on inside and have some coffee and tell me what all this is about.'

It was then that Lee noticed the small valise lashed to the saddle-horn of Lea's pony. A question was in his mind but he refrained from voicing it. Instead, he untied the rope and lifted the valise down.

At that moment, Jesse came out on to the gallery, a lantern in his hand. He set down the lantern and tramped down the steps to where Lee stood with the girl.

He smiled. 'Figgered I heard voices–'

'This is Lea Franchot – Jesse Rust,' Kells said. 'Lea's a good friend of mine from Hide City.'

'Any friend of yours is welcome, Lee, though we ain't got much here in the way of comfort.'

'Thank you, Jesse,' Lea's voice was low, more controlled now. 'Don't worry about me.'

'I'll put up your horse and give it a feed,'

Jesse said catching up the trailing reins.

Kells took the girl by the arm and firmly but gently propelled her up the steps and into the house, leading her to the entrance of the living-room.

'Wait while I get a light,' he told her.

He crossed the darkened room to the table on which a shaded lamp stood.

Lea heard the match being struck and then the sulphur flared and she watched from the doorway as Kells adjusted the wick and replaced the chimney.

'I'm afraid the place is a bit bare, Lea,' he apologised. 'We haven't had much time to think about adding more furniture.'

She came towards him, making an impatient, almost imperious gesture with her hand. He saw, in the lamplight, that without heavy make-up, she was more beautiful than before. She had slipped the cloak from her shoulders and her jet black hair was a dark frame to the pallor of her cheeks.

He indicated a battered sofa and she sank down gratefully on the worn leather seat.

'Stay right there while I fix you some coffee, Lea.'

She smiled faintly. 'I'm not likely to get up and run away after ridin' for a day and a night to get here.'

Bill Rust already had the coffee-pot on the stove, Jesse having told him about their late visitor. Shortly, Lee came back with two cups of steaming java.

Lea sipped the stimulating drink and presently placed the cup on the floor beside her.

'Lee,' she said earnestly. 'I had to come and warn you. Frank Shane's in Hide City; came with a trail of beef. He's plannin' to attack you, right here on – on what's this place? Yes; Clayton's Strip.'

'How did you hear all this, Lea?' Kells shaped and lit a cigarette, his eyes on the girl's face. There was a subtle change about Lea Franchot he thought, something quite apart from her clothes and appearance.

'They came into the Silver Dollar as they nearly always do. Like I told you, Lee. I overheard Frank and Cal Beston plannin' to attack this place on Clayton's Strip. He's gettin' some more gunmen from Hide City. Two of the Arrow riders brought in new hands while I was listening behind the partition of the booth.'

'More gunmen, eh? Well that's news.'

Lea's eyes clouded. 'You mean that the other isn't news to you? You mean you knew he was plannin' all this?'

Kells got up and walked over to the sofa. There was an unusual warmth in his eyes, a softness in his voice, as he spoke.

'We guessed some of it, Lea. But that doesn't make any difference to the fact you've ridden all this way to warn us. That's one of the reasons we're putting up a fence round the house.' He paused. 'If there was some way to show you how grateful I am for your help – it must have been a hell of a chore riding day and night. Weren't you scared?'

She gave a wan kind of smile.

'Scared as hell, Lee. I lost my way several times but decided the best thing to do was to make for Lordville.'

He nodded his agreement of her reasoning.

'Fortunately for me I met up with the sheriff. He was damned suspicious at first – a woman on her own wanderin' about at night – but I convinced him I was a friend of yours and that I had to find you.'

'What then?' Kells asked and then, suddenly remembering, shaped and lit a cigarette, handing it to the girl.

Her eyes thanked him. 'I guess Arnold – that's his name isn't it? – is an all-right hombre. He insisted on saddlin' up and ridin' most of the way from Lordville with me, but I was still uncertain this was the place. I guess I've got a suspicious nature.'

'I'd say,' Kells remarked thoughtfully, 'that your job in Hide City has given you every reason to be suspicious and question the motives of most folk.'

'Perhaps so, Lee. Anyway I'm quit of it now. I've left Art Lucas.'

Kells's thick brows lifted. 'Wasn't he mad?'

'I didn't dare tell him! I left a note and skipped out. I was in a hurry to get away from Art, you can bet, as well as wantin' to get here fast and warn you.'

'That's why you've brought a valise,' Lee said slowly and then asked. 'What are you going to do, Lea?'

She sat contemplating the glowing end of the quirly for a long moment, as though fascinated by the upward curling smoke.

'I have a brother in New Mexico Territory. I know whereabouts he is, so I figured to join him.' She smiled up at Kells and he wondered why her eyes were suddenly blurred and misty. If she were gong home to her brother – if she were quitting Hide City and Texas, for good, surely it was a cause for smiles rather than tears?

'Anyway, I'm glad I came,' she said presently, 'even if you did know most what Shane was plannin'. Is he – is he, after all…?'

'He's the man I've been after for ten years,' Kells said soberly. 'He's Frank Shards all right from the San Saba Valley and he knows who I am.'

She arose and placed a hand on Kells' arm. 'I hope you make out all right, Lee. I'll be gone before Arrow gets here.'

'It's getting late, Lea. If you can catch some sleep on the sofa I'll rustle you up some blankets.' His gaze was anxiously on her face as though this were a poor enough return for what she had done.

She smiled and nodded. 'This'll do me fine, Lee...'

Early next morning, the men again sweated blood fighting the springy bob-wire, cutting and nailing it from post to post.

'We shall need another couple of coils,' Kells grunted presently, 'and that means one of us breaking off and riding into town.'

Lea, standing on the gallery, said, 'I'll go, Lee, just so's there's some way I can haul it back.'

Lee straightened up and nodded. 'Joe Ward's boy'll haul it out. You can ride back with Ward's spring wagon.'

He left the coil of wire he had been cutting and walked across the yard towards her.

'I'll saddle your pony, Lea.'

She followed him into the dim interior of the stable, watching him as he threw on blanket and saddle. Her eyes must have held something of her feelings for when Kells straightened up from buckling the surcingle, he held still a moment, caught up by the glimpse of dreams in back of that wistful gaze.

He turned abruptly, almost awkwardly, from bridling the paint, looking down at her whilst he looped the reins over his arm.

But Lea would not, could not help him. If there were anything in a man's heart at all, it could only be transposed into words because of his own spontaneous and urgent need. Lea was wise enough to sense and understand that unless the feeling were there, any attempt to probe would be useless and futile anyway.

Outside the barn she turned quickly and mounted. Her voice, when she spoke was purposely flat. 'Be seein' you, Lee, and I'll make it as fast as I can.'

He nodded and smiled as she made towards the river and like any woman in love she cherished that farewell smile and hugged its memory, reading into it a significance worthy of something better than the meagre offering it was...

Lee came back to the ranch yard and spoke at once to Jesse.

'There's only enough wire now for a couple of us to work on, Jesse. It might be a good time to move the cattle.'

Jesse nodded. 'You figure two of us can work them?'

'If the going's not too rough and the canyon's close to hand.'

'An ideal spot,' Jessie grinned, 'and only a coupla miles from the big pasture.'

Lee nodded and explained to Bill Rust and Yerby what they proposed to do.

'I could haze that herd o' critturs single-handed if it meant quittin' this goddam' fencin' for a spell,' Yerby grumbled.

Lee's face relaxed sufficiently to show a grin. 'We'll be back by noon or thereabouts, Bill. Then you can take a spell while Jesse and me finish the good work.'

With that Bill Rust and Yerby had to be content as they re-applied themselves to the task most hateful to all waddies.

But Kells and Jesse Rust were not back by noon. The ground over which the ninety head of cattle had to be hazed towards the canyon, was more broken and rocky than Jesse Rust had remembered.

Some of the shale slopes were steep enough to cause dogies to slide stiff-legged for yards at a time and hoofs and legs were often gashed by sharp upthrust shale and stone.

The steers didn't like this kind of trail at all and had to be almost literally pushed as coiled lariats pounded the reluctant rumps of the drag steers.

It had been nine o'clock when they had set out from Oak-leaf for the fenced pasture. By the time the sweating men had got the stubborn herd safely corralled in the 'hidden' canyon, the sun showed it was about four o'clock.

'Well we made it, Jesse. Even though we are a mite late on our schedule.'

Jesse Rust nodded and grinned through the dust and sweat caking his face. He pulled out a red handkerchief and wiped his face and hands, nodding towards the cattle now contentedly grazing on the short, brown, sun-cured grass.

'They won't shift from there anyway. Good summer grass and water further along.'

Kells sat his horse as he surveyed the narrow entrance to the canyon, and tiredly built a cigarette.

'Well, Jesse, whatever happens at Oak-leaf, I'd take a bet that Arrow won't find them in a hurry.'

Rust nodded, sobered by Lee's reference to Arrow and by the thought of what lay ahead of them.

'Let's go,' Lee said presently and both men wheeled their mounts, pointing them towards the ranch house...

They came through the open section of the fence just as Yerby and the younger Rust were setting the gate on its hinges. The last strand of bob-wire had been fixed and the two Bills, half dead on their feet, surveyed their handiwork with open pride, cocking enquiring eyebrows at Jesse and Lee for their approbation.

Jesse said. 'A swell job, men. Wait'll we start payin' out bonuses.' He turned to Lee. 'I'll strip and water your hoss along with mine.'

Kells threw him the reins as his glance lifted to the gallery. Lea was coming towards them bearing a tray and glasses.

Lee's gaze moved over to Yerby, who grinned widely.

'She surely is an angel, Lee. You wait'll you see what's goin' in them glasses.'

Lea Franchot smiled, setting the tray down on a box in the shade of a single sycamore. She turned back to the house without a word and returned almost immediately carrying too heavily weighted lard pails. Lee moved quickly towards her, taking the pails from her in silent wonderment. Each pail was half-filled with ice and above that, necks thrust down, were a half-dozen or so bottles of – beer.

'Beer! Ice-cold at that!' Yerby grinned catching up a pail from Kells and setting it in the shade.

'Lea's jest about saved our lives to-day,' Yerby rambled on. 'What it is to have a woman about the house.'

'You haul the ice in from town?' Kells said.

She nodded. 'I had to wait awhile for the Ward's wagon. Henry was out someplace with it. I got to thinking of these boys sweating out here in the sun all day so I got around Race Arnold to get the beer and together we filled the pails with ice.

'It's sure meltin' now, but it's chilled the liquor well enough.'

'Why, Lea. That's a right smart idea,' Kells drawled. 'Reckon I'd like a sample of that myself.'

'Comin' up, sir!' Lea smiled unstoppering a bottle and pouring the cool, foaming liquid into a glass...

Chapter Sixteen

ARROW'S HERE

Lamplight in the kitchen gleamed brightly on the red check table-cloth, which was another of Lea's touches. She had not wasted time during her wait in town, neither had she been idle on her return to Oak-leaf, as Bill Rust bore witness.

'Small wonder you've all emptied the stew-pot,' he said, 'considerin' Miss Lea did the cookin'.'

Lea gave him her smiling glance. 'You helped, Bill–'

'Me?' he grinned. 'I jest pared the vegetables and got in the way.'

Kells built a cigarette, started to scrape a match across the table-cloth and quickly transferred it to the sole of his boot. He met Lea's sly glance of amusement and unaccountably his face coloured.

In the living-room, Kells set the logs blazing in the hearth against the chill of the night air. He fetched another lamp and lit it,

244

turning as footsteps sounded from the kitchen and came to a stop at the entrance to the room.

Lea had changed from riding costume to more feminine garb. Her dress was of velvet, the colour of claret, a darkly brilliant tone which offset the smooth whiteness of neck and shoulders only partly revealed.

The black hair was drawn back, almost to a degree of severity and caught by a single velvet ribbon of matching shade.

For perhaps the first time Kells saw her, not as a saloon girl, not as the ex-mistress of Art Lucas, but as a lovely young woman.

Here was some kind of transformation, some subtle change which he had sensed before, and yet, still found baffling. It was not merely her clothes. Lea herself, he thought, in some strangely elusive way, has changed.

She moved forwards into the room, flushing with pleasure at what she read into his gaze. What did it matter if he refused to phrase his thoughts into pretty compliments? Kells was just not that kind of man...

He asked as he shaped and lit another cigarette, 'Have you had coffee, Lea?'

She shook her head. 'No, neither have you. I'll get some from the kitchen.'

Lee grunted and seated himself on a packing-case in this bare, ill-furnished room. There was no holding the woman, he thought.

She came back in a few moments and handed Kells his cup.

'We're all set now, Lea, but I figure you ought to be gone by now. Frank may jump us at any time from now on.'

She nodded. 'I made enquiries at the stage office in town. There's a coach leavin' at eight to-morrow. I've booked a seat.'

'How far does it go?'

She rested her chin on the heel of her hand and frowned. 'Let's see. The stage'll take me as far as Cottonwood. I'm told it's a long ride. From there I can get a train. Guess that will take two-three days. Then another stage and then I'll be at Sage Flats – I hope.'

'What about your horse, Lea? Did you rent it from the livery in Hide City?'

She shook her head. 'No, it's not a rented one. Sellars, I think, had figured out what I was doin' and offered me the paint at an absurd price.'

'I see. Well, what are you going to do about him. It's a cinch you can't load him in a box-car all the way to New Mexico.'

She gazed at him out of level eyes in which, paradoxically there seemed to be a hint of laughter.

'I've thought of all that, Lee, and I'd like for you to have him as a kind of – well, keepsake.'

Lee shook his head. 'I couldn't take your

paint, Lea. He's a wonderful animal. You could sell him for seventy dollars. God-damit!' he suddenly exploded, 'aren't I indebted to you enough already?' He got up and began to pace the room. 'First you stake me, a complete stranger, because you figure, rightly too, I'm down to my last silver piece. Thanks to you and the roulette wheel I come out of the saloon with a tidy pokeful of cash.

'Not content with that,' Kells continued almost angrily, 'you ride day and night to warn me that Frank Shards is hiring more gunmen and intends to smash this place on Clayton's Strip and me along with it. Now you want to give me your horse as a – what was it you said? Yeah! A keepsake!'

She watched the hot anger slowly ebb from this man who was normally so un-moved by anything other than his lust for personal vengeance.

She rose from the couch and placed a hand, gently, on his arm in the same sort of gesture that a mother might extend to an over-fretful child.

'I'm sorry, Lea. I told you before I was damned ornery and an ungrateful cuss. You see–'

Crack! They both stood rigid as the gun-blast from somewhere out in the darkness shattered through Kells words. Lea was standing near the window and as Kells moved forwards towards the nearest lamp, the sound of voices cut through the echoing after-silence of the gunshot.

Lee thought he recognised Jesse's voice and then came the crash of a gate being closed tightly.

Another gun opened up as Lee extinguished the nearer lamp inside the living-room.

Boots pounded along the corridor as the door burst open. Bill Yerby stood there, breathing hard, a smoking carbine in his hand. 'Douse the lights! Arrow's here!'

Lee streaked across the room and seemingly only then remembered to warn Lea.

'Get to hell away from that window!'

As Kells' hand fumbled with the wick-wheel of the second lamp, Lea moved forward, right into the path of a bullet which smashed itself through the window.

And as the room was plunged into darkness, Lee heard her low cry and leaped forward, half catching her, breaking her fall to the boards.

He cursed quietly and bitterly, vaguely aware of the mounting crescendo of noise outside. Guns were opening up now from somewhere in the house; the kitchen windows he figured as he quickly gathered the limp figure in his arms and groped his way to the partly open door.

Yerby had not waited and Kells judged that after his brief warning he had gone to join the Rust brothers.

Kells paused at the doorway, seeing the glow ahead from the low burning lamp in the passage way. The living-room would be left unguarded, was his bleak thought as he moved with his burden towards the further bedroom.

He laid her gently on the bed before drawing the thick gunny-sack curtains. He had to risk a light and as he exploded a match holding it to the lamp and turning the wick low, he realised the choice he had to make.

Either he could leave Lea right here, hoping for the best, so that he could weigh in with his own gun, or else–.His mouth hardened into a thin line. If he tended Lea now, the chances were that Arrow would break through in spite of the fence and kill every one of them in the ranch house.

For a second, Lee hesitated. He raised his head, seeking to identify in his mind the various guns which were now filling the night air and to discover from where the Rust boys and Yerby were directing their fire.

He moved quickly from the bedroom to the kitchen door. The Rust boys were inside, dark shapes silhouetted against a less intense background.

'Lea's been hit!' Kells' voice sounded harsh. 'Hold them off Jesse until I can lend a hand.'

Jesse nodded and cursed as a bullet exploded in the window-frame, showering him with slivers of glass, cutting his face and hands so that blood appeared simultaneously in a dozen places.

'You bloody bastards,' he whispered and levered a fresh shell, sighting carefully. He fired and almost immediately a man's curse and scream rose above the noise of conflict. From the other window, Bill Rust carefully made a chalk-mark on the wall.

'Yerby's in the small room, covering the back, Lee,' Jesse said, wiping blood from his face. 'Can you cover us from the living room?'

'Just as soon as I've fixed Lea—'

'She ain't daid, Lee?'

'She's breathing,' Kells said. 'That's all I know right now. That and the fact that Frank's got even more to answer for now.'

He moved back out of the room, hearing Yerby's carbine speak for the first time from the small rear room, as he groped his way back to the bedroom, stopping only to grab a clean bandana and a bottle half full of whisky.

In the soft lamplight, he tore at the fastenings of Lea's dress. Her rasping breath goaded him unmercifully as he stripped the material away from under her left arm, to reveal the white flesh, now made ugly and

250

bloody by a gunman's bullet.

He felt her back carefully and could discover no outlet with his probing fingers. That meant the bullet was still inside her.

For the moment all he could do was to cleanse the raw mouth of the wound and wad and bind it tightly to stop the alarming flow of blood.

The grim task was completed in a matter of minutes. Kells' face was wooden as he looked down on that pale, set face.

'I'll be in again to see you, Lea,' he told the unconscious girl. 'Don't go and die, lady.' He felt a strange constriction in his throat as he emerged from the room, groping for his carbine against the wall of the passage.

He knew it was fully loaded, as always, and now as he moved softly through the living-room, he levered the first of ten shells into the breech.

He pushed the battered sofa against the window wall and knelt on the seat. This way he could fire more easily and at the same time the sofa afforded some extra protection.

The Winchester's muzzle poked through the already broken glass. Across the yard, beyond the fence, Kells could see the blurred shapes of riders.

Here and there an orange flame stabbed the starlit night and slugs screamed on their wild errand of death. So far, at least, Arrow had not got through the fence into the yard.

Kells wondered grimly how long it would be before one of them produced a pair of wire-cutters. He could hear Frank Shards' voice raised in anger above the din of gunfire.

A shadowy figure was by the gate, fumbling with the bar, or perhaps even cutting at the wire. Lee could not see clearly enough to be sure. His glance ran down the Winchester's barrel to the forward sight. He moved the carbine a fraction, drawing a steady bead on the man at the gate.

The scream and the carbine's explosion seemed almost simultaneous as Kells saw the figure stagger, half spin round and then slide down the gate-post to the ground. At least two or three Arrow men must have been hit, Kells thought, and found possible confirmation of this in the sudden slackening off of fire from beyond.

On a sudden impulse, Lee came off the sofa, running in a half-crouch from the room into the passage way and out through the gallery door. He was on the porch now, in pitch-black darkness, immune from anything but a chance bullet until he should make his presence known.

The firing was still only desultory, more coming from the ranch itself than from the attackers.

Kells lifted his voice so that it would carry to beyond the fence where Frank was urging his men to fresh efforts. 'I've got no fight with you Arrow men,' Lee called. 'My quarrel's with Frank out there. What are you getting yourselves shot up for?'

Frank's angry voice cut in before Kells could do more damage with his verbal ammunition. Already some of the Arrow riders were exchanging meaningful glances and three of the men lay on the ground, one cursing obscenely, the other two ominously silent.

'You throw down your guns and come on out with your hands up, Kells,' Shards bellowed, 'else we'll blast the lot of you to hell-and-be-merry. We ain't got any quarrel with the Rust boys—'

'Like hell, you haven't!' Kells' voice was charged with scorn. 'You only rustled their stock so's you could start in moving Arrow beef across the Strip and out to the northeast.'

All firing had stopped now and the very air seemed charged with the violent hatred of man for man. Now, in a sudden upsurge of resolve, Kells had irrevocably decided upon his course. He dropped the Winchester on to a seat and emerged from the shadows of the porch clearly showing himself for the first time.

'I'm coming for you, Frank Shards, and I'm warning your crew to keep out of this. Maybe they don't know you lynched my father back in the San Saba Valley. If they did, I doubt whether any of them would fire another gun for you.' Kells was walking steadily towards the fence all the time he spoke. He was running a bluff, trading on his knowledge of such men that whilst he talked and supplied them with these surprising facts, they would not move against him. He was also flattering their egos and what finer instincts some of them possessed. Charlie Heyman, Ray Lusgow and Phil Dukes noticeably drew away from Frank and kept their hands in full view.

'That's a lie!' Shards screamed, 'a dam' lie!'

'No!' Kells cut in. 'It's no lie, Frank and you know it' – here Kells ran another bluff – 'what's more I've got proof you're Frank Shards – and witnesses.'

'What if I am Frank Shards?' the Arrow owner screamed. 'I didn't do it. I didn't do it I tell you–' He was almost babbling now; half crazy with fear and bitter rage, as in one half-despairing gesture he suddenly turned and went for his gun.

Kells' six-gun was already out, but before even the trigger-slack could be taken in, a Colt boomed out from behind the Arrow men and Frank Shards alias Frank Shane spun round, six-shooter half-drawn from leather.

Two of the transfixed group stirred themselves and dived for guns, but a hard voice spoke from the shadows of the live-oaks.

'Hold it, you men! First one as goes for his gun gets it in the guts.'

From the belt of trees a slight figure emerged; grey hair showed faintly in the starlight from beneath the pushed back stetson. A five-pointed star glittered on the calf-skin vest as Sheriff Race Arnold moved slowly forward, a smoking gun held firm and steady in his fist.

Kells felt as though his very life-blood were draining away. For a brief moment his mind examined the possibility that he had been hit. He started to walk the last few yards towards the gate and sensed that this almost light-headed feeling was due to the shocking reaction.

For ten years he had hunted this man and now when at last he had him in his gun-sights, vengeance was snatched from him by this almost insignificant lawman.

The objective side of Kells' brain recognised, even in that tense moment, Arnold's superb shot in the starlit night.

The Arrow men were no longer grim-faced gunmen; they backed down, not only in the face of Kells' and Arnold's guns, but in face of this sudden stark killing on the part of Race Arnold.

The sheriff's grey glance lifted to Kells' face. 'It was my chore, after all, son.'

'To hell with that!' Kells snarled. 'It was my pa he murdered and I'm Ezra Kells' son.'

Phil Dukes spoke up then and it was as if he voiced the question that was turning over in the minds of all those Arrow gunmen.

'Did he really do that, Kells? Was his name Shards like you said?'

Slowly, Kells sheathed his gun and as slowly wiped his hand down the leg of his levis in a purely instinctive yet unconscious gesture.

Kells told them then the whole story in brief, clipped sentences. There was not one man who did not look a little sheepish and a little ashamed. Such is the mood of the herd; bloody violence turned suddenly to a receptive humility.

Arnold moved over to Kells and stood before him, looking up into that dark, bleak face.

'Vengeance alone is no good, Kells, believe me. Always before you have only killed in self-defence, because it has been forced on you—'

'This was common justice,' Lee said stonily.

Arnold's head moved slowly from side to side. 'One of these days, Lee, you'll thank me for this night's work. Not now, perhaps, but later.'

He turned to Phil Dukes who seemed to

be the appointed spokesman of Arrow. 'You going to load these men on their mounts and pull back to Arrow?'

There was no threat in Arnold's voice. It was just a simple question that he was asking.

Dukes' glance touched each man in turn. None of them moved or so much as nodded a head, but Dukes read their answer clearly enough.

'We're pulling out, sheriff, back to Arrow.'

Kells turned to meet Yerby and Jesse walking towards him.

'We heard most of it, Lee,' Bill said. 'It's all over now. Come inside for a drink.'

While Jesse stayed outside on his watching brief, Lee and Yerby returned to the house, the latter going round with matches and a lantern, lighting the lamps.

Kells stood looking down at the girl on the bed, noting her shallow breathing. He reached for the whisky bottle and half-drained it at a single gulp. The room rocked round and then stood still and as Kells wiped the back of his hand across his mouth, it was as though something within him suddenly righted itself and like the room, slipped into its correct perspective.

'Bill,' Kells called and the younger Rust boy appeared in the doorway, 'Jesse is out in the yard, Bill,' Kells said. 'Get him to tell the sheriff to get Doc Ivory over here and make it fast.'

'Okay, Lee.' Bill Rust slipped quietly away on his errand.

Kells reached over and took Lea's limp hand. The lamp was turned high now and he could even see the slow pulse beating in her neck. He put the whisky to her lips, placing his arm around her shoulders and raising her head from the pillow.

'Drink this, honey, it'll do you good.'

The words were only whispered yet some soft urgency about them seemed to communicate itself to the girl.

Her lips moved slightly and her teeth came unclenched so that Lee was able to feed her a drop or two of the spirit.

She managed to swallow some, gagged a little, then took some more. The soot-black eye-lashes fluttered apart as she gazed up into Lee's anxious face.

'You called me "honey" just now,' she whispered in a faint voice shaded with wonder.

'Sure I did,' Kells said. 'But I'll call you a dam' sight worse names than that if you don't hurry up and get better *pronto*.'

'I'm better now,' she murmured closing her eyes and holding Kells hand tightly in her own...

Chapter Seventeen

LETTIE COMES WITH US

It had been late, very late, when quiet had at last enveloped Oak-leaf ranch house.

Kells had sat beside Lea's bed after Bill Yerby had helped to move her into the small rear room. Perhaps they shouldn't have tried moving her at all was Lee's nagging thought, as he watched the mask of sweat slowly appear on that pale tight face.

Hoof-beats and the crunch of wheels in the yard told Kells that the medico had at last arrived and in a few moments Doc Ivory entered the room. He nodded briefly to Kells and pulled back the blankets from Lea's body.

Kells' bleak gaze remained fixed on the medico's face whilst Ivory made his careful examination. When he finally straightened up from the bed Kells had his moment of sick fear, such a feeling as he had not experienced since that night in the San Saba Valley.

Yet there were other feelings, deep down inside him, which stirred momentarily in his breast before they too slipped quietly away, like the spirit of Lea Franchot, into the tranquil nirvana of infinity…

Kells did not need to hear the medico's words, or even to read the message in his eyes, as Ivory quietly covered the still form on the bed, extending the blanket so that it completely masked the waxen face and dark, shining hair…

By the time Ivory's buggy had clattered through the yard and the now open gate, the palest glimmer of grey showed in the eastern sky. Earlier, at Lee's suggestion, the Rust brothers and Yerby had turned in to snatch some sleep. Now Kells washed up at the pump in the yard, his mind so occupied that he was unaware of the cold water and the chill of early dawn on his half-naked body.

He returned to the house and lit the stove, restlessly pacing the kitchen until the coffee started bubbling on the stove top.

He poured a cup and rolled and lit a cigarette, gazing out of the shattered windows at the lightening range with unseeing eyes.

Already he was beginning to think that perhaps Race Arnold had been right. He was reminded now of something his father had once said and full recollection came flooding back to him now, even though he had chosen to forget it over the years. '"Vengeance is mine", saith the Lord,' Old Ezra had quoted him in the far distant nester's cabin on the verge of the Crockett Spread.

Yes! Lee had elected not to remember it all

these years, caught up as he had been in that bitter thirst for revenge on his father's killer. 'Just retribution' he had termed it, but a retribution far greater than any Kells could mete out had overtaken Frank Shards. It had been a lawman's gun, rightly so, that had finally fired the bullet and dealt out the harsh justice of this lawless land...

It was the second afternoon since that memorable fight; since Lea Franchot had stopped the bullet intended for Kells and, as a result had quietly died. Yesterday, they had brought a spring wagon in from town and Lea's blanket-covered form had been gently lowered into the bed of the wagon.

'I'll handle this, Lee,' Bill Yerby had said and for once Kells had been thankful to obey rather than give orders.

Now the sound of hoof-beats echoed through the warm afternoon and Lee, coming out on to the gallery saw Anna Collier dismounting and hitching her horse to the tie-rail out front.

He came down the steps to greet her; his face less wooden than before.

Anna smiled. 'I tried to get here before, Lee, as soon as I heard—'

He took her hand and held it a moment. 'Come on to the gallery and talk to me.'

'That's just why I came. That and to see—' she blushed furiously, and Kells smiled for the first time in two days. 'Jesse Rust,' he finished gently.

They sat in the battered rockers and presently Bill Yerby's round face thrust itself round the door.

'Howdy, Anna,' he grinned. 'You want some Oak-leaf cawffee?'

'I'd sure admire some,' she laughed.

'Make it two cups, Bill,' Lee said building a smoke.

Anna watched Kells' hands as he shaped the quirly and wiped a match alight.

'Arnold told me to tell you he's arranging for Lea's funeral in two days, Lee. It's all over town, of course, how she–'

Lee nodded soberly. 'You know, Anna, I believe she's happier now, where she is–' He broke off, startled and confused at having tried to put his secret thoughts into words.

Anna smiled gently. 'I understand, Lee, and I think you're right.' She gave him a long searching look. 'Lea wouldn't have been happy if she had lived, Lee.'

His gaze was straight ahead, subconsciously taking in the details of the wire fence, the range beyond.

'Because of me?' he asked quietly.

'It was all or nothing with Lea,' Anna replied, 'but then I guess most women are like that.' She cleared her throat; it was merely symbolic of changing the subject.

'Race Arnold says he figures Arrow

belongs to me now Lee. What do you think?'

Kells nodded slowly. 'It's a cinch. Frank had no other relatives and if he did we're sure not going to start looking for 'em. You're now the owner of the biggest spread in the territory.'

'What am I going to do, Lee?'

'You mean about the ranch? How you are going to run it?'

She nodded and, surprisingly, Kells suddenly grinned down at her.

'There's a man inside there–' he jerked his thumb in the direction of the ranch house, 'name's Jesse Rust. He's been called a "damned rawhider". He's not much more'n a boy but I'd say he was a man to tie to, Anna. A man to ride the river with.'

He saw a slow flush stain her cheeks and a sparkle appear in her eyes.

Yerby emerged from the house and set coffee-cups on the rickety table.

'How's it feel to be a big ranch owner, Anna?' he grinned.

'I don't know yet, Bill. Looks like one of the first chores'll be to find some riders.'

Lee said. 'I've already ridden over to Arrow, yesterday, when – when they were taking Lea into town. I figured to get a few things settled.'

'Tell me.'

Lee drank some of his coffee and replaced the table. 'Frank brought four new hands with him from Hide City. Gunmen, of course, to replace those that had gone; Foley Kessel, Luke Putnam, Zip Cantrell killed and later, Schillinger.'

'Schillinger? I didn't know.'

'He jumped me with a gun when I rode over to see whether Frank was still there or with the trail-herd. A horse saved my life and I got the drop on George.' Lee told her then what had happened.

'Frank must have ridden back from Hide City with his crew, saw Schillinger dead and then lit out, right away with his riders to attack us here.'

'Who were killed?'

'Cal Beston and two of the new gunnies. Eddie Hindel died later from his wounds–'

'It's terrible,' Anna whispered.

Kells nodded. 'But it's over now. Things will be different from now on in Creation Valley. I gave Phil Dukes, Sol Schultz and Rayner Lusgow the chance to stay on and sent the rest packing. I figured you wouldn't mind.'

'Mind? I'm grateful, Lee, for what you've done and glad you sent those others away. I always thought that Ray, Phil and Schultz were not so bad as the rest.'

'They're rough-and-tumble men, Anna, but none of them cottoned much to out-and-out murder. They just stayed with Frank because they – well, habit's a hard thing to cut loose from.'

She nodded. 'Since you're organising things for me, Lee, who's going to rod the spread and where'll I get some more riders?'

Lee caught the sparkle of mischief in her eyes and grinned.

'I'd say that Jesse Rust would be a good enough hand to ramrod Arrow for you. As for a *segundo,* well, Race Arnold's got a sick wife and three kids. His county pay's not enough and he's got time to spare. Also he's a first-rate cow-puncher.'

She gazed at him wide-eyed. 'You sure have got things worked out, Lee. But what about yourself?'

He shrugged. 'Me and Yerby and Bill Rust will be staying on with Oak-leaf.'

Anna said with apparently complete irrelevance. 'How's Marion Starr going to make out? If I'm going to take over Arrow, I shall have to quit helping her.'

Kells looked at her in silent amazement and should have been warned by the look in back of her eyes.

'What do you mean, Anna? What's it got to do with me?'

She said mischievously. 'As you seemed to have got everything else figured out, I thought maybe you would have found a solution for Marion's problems.'

'Who are you kidding?' Kells said, half-suspiciously.

Anna's expression sobered. 'I'm not kidding any one, Lee. Least of all you. But Marion's a wonderful cook and – it looks like you could do with one at Oak-leaf!' she added wickedly.

Bill Rust had put up Anna's horse in the barn and as dusk fell, Oak-leaf's triangle sent up its harsh clanging to summon them for the evening meal.

Kells was reminded of the time two nights ago, when Oak-leaf had sat around the kitchen table for the evening meal. Lea's check cloth; Lea herself, lovely in the lamplight; Jesse and Bill Rust, grim-faced; Yerby casual and confident.

But to-night things were vastly changed. Anna Collier sat at Lea's place and her gaze was more often on Jesse's face than in front of her. Jesse, too, was like a love-sick calf and Yerby grinned broadly at the side-play.

Kells rose abruptly as soon as he had finished and Anna said. 'If you are going into town Lee, perhaps you would tell Marion the news. Say I'll be back to thank her and collect my things.'

Lee's jaw dropped as he looked down at the expression of bland innocence on Anna's face.

'How in hell – I mean how did you know I was figuring on riding into town, Anna?'

She smiled serenely. 'Call it a woman's intuition if you like. Anyway you do need a woman to look after you. Bill's a fair good cook but it's not quite the same—' Anna broke off and had the grace to blush and Kells beat a hasty retreat from the room.

He walked to the stable, lit the hanging lantern and saddled up before he even realised what he was doing...

He rode slowly to Lordville, thinking about what Anna had said and particularly what she had left unsaid. He thought about Lea, too; the feeling of guilt which he had experienced since the moment she had been shot was now quickly vanishing like a racing rider who becomes fast swallowed up in his own dust-cloud.

The mental picture of Lea's face, likewise, was little more than a blurred shape and he suddenly knew that whatever attraction he had felt for the girl had been merely physical and illusory.

The old haunting moods had been completely discarded by the time he reached town. No more did he feel bitterness against Race Arnold for robbing him of vengeance, and no more did he feel anything for Lea save a quiet content that she had found peace...

He racked the horse outside Starr's, amid the bustle and activity of evening traffic, and pushed open the screen door of the restaurant.

It was nearing nine o'clock and most of

Marion Starr's customers had already eaten and had departed for saloons, poker-games and even business meetings.

Lettie was serving a few late eaters with coffee, and smiled quickly at him, indicating the kitchen with a backward fling of her head.

Kells tramped through and saw Marion kneeling before the stove, a last tray of cookies in her hands. He watched the lamplight play on the red-brown hair and admired the flush on her cheeks and the soft curve of her neck.

She looked up suddenly as he moved into the room, and the faint flash of alarm which had sprung to her eyes was erased by the welcoming smile which lit her whole face.

'Howdy, Lee,' she said. 'Be with you in a minute. Sit down and I'll fix you some coffee. Would you like something to eat?'

Lee smiled. 'A woman after my own heart. Always ready to rustle up food and drink for a man.'

She laid the tray of cookies on top of the stove, wiped her hands on the flour-sack apron and poured two cups of coffee.

'It's a purely mercenary instinct, I assure you, Lee.' She laughed a little shakily. 'Don't forget I make my living from food and coffee.'

Kells nodded. But he had seen the warm light in her eyes, had glimpsed something else, deeper down, if he were not mistaken.

'I had a meal Marion, though I reckon I ought to have patronised you more than I have done. Things have been kind of busy.'

'I know,' she agreed, seating herself at the opposite end of the table. 'You don't have to say it, Lee. How glad I am that the trouble is over now; that there will be no more killings, no more suffering. Lea Franchot must have been a – a wonderful sort of girl.'

'I guess she was,' Kells said quietly. 'And I think she's happy now.' He drank some coffee and presently gave her Anna's message.

'It looks like your hired hands have done let you down, Marion,' Kells smiled.

'I don't mind, just so long as Anna's happy with her Jesse. I'm glad, terribly glad for her sake.'

'You know,' Kells said, 'you're rather a wonderful woman yourself, though it looks like no one's found time to say so – or have they?'

She shook her head and smiled. The dancing light was back in her eyes. 'So long as you've found the time–' she began.

He stood up abruptly and Marion, too, pushed her chair back, following suit.

'Do you really mean that?' he said softly.

'Ever since you first came to Lordville – how long is it, two-three weeks? – you've been the only one whose good opinion I care about, Lee.'

She stood straight before him, arms hanging easily at her sides, perfectly relaxed. The sincerity in her words and voice was mirrored in her eyes.

Kells said: 'Would you sell out here and – and come to Oak-leaf as my wife?'

She still regarded him steadily with that straight-browed, level gaze. 'If you wanted me to take a covered wagon to Oregon, the answer would be the same.'

'Yes?' he asked softly.

'Yes!'

She was in his arms then, holding him tightly, her warm mouth brushing his lips and covering his face with kisses that made his head swim.

She looked up into his face whilst his arms were still around her, and he saw the question in back of her radiant eyes.

He nodded gently. 'Sure, Marion,' he agreed, 'Lettie comes with us.'

The publishers hope that this book has given you enjoyable reading. Large Print Books are especially designed to be as easy to see and hold as possible. If you wish a complete list of our books please ask at your local library or write directly to:

The Golden West Large Print Books
Magna House, Long Preston,
Skipton, North Yorkshire.
BD23 4ND

This Large Print Book, for people
who cannot read normal print,
is published under the auspices of

THE ULVERSCROFT FOUNDATION

... we hope you have enjoyed this book.
Please think for a moment about those
who have worse eyesight than you ...
and are unable to even read or enjoy
Large Print without great difficulty.

You can help them by sending a
donation, large or small, to:

**The Ulverscroft Foundation,
1, The Green, Bradgate Road,
Anstey, Leicestershire, LE7 7FU,
England.**
or request a copy of our brochure for
more details.

The Foundation will use all donations
to assist those people who are visually
impaired and need special attention
with medical research, diagnosis
and treatment.

Thank you very much for your help.